Moving North

Book One • Perryside Series

Tudor Robins

Other Books by Tudor Robins:

All-Ages Books:

Stolen Saddles (Book One – Mystery Stables)

Gift Horse (Holiday Novella)

Books for Readers 12 and Up:

Island Series

Six-Month Horse (Prequel)

Appaloosa Summer (Book One)

Wednesday Riders (Book Two)

Join Up (Book Three)

Faults (Book Four)

Reason Why (Book Five)

Stonegate Series

Objects in Mirror (Book One)

After Lucas (Book Two)

Throw Your Heart Over (Book Three)

Perryside Series

Moving North (Book One)

Stand-Alone

Meant to Be (Young Adult)

Books for Readers Over 16:

Before & After (Women's Fiction)

Not so Bad (Women's Fiction / Small-Town Romance)

In Search Of (Small-Town Romance)

Chapter One

It's our second funeral in six months.

The good thing about that is Lief's dark pants, and the black sneakers we bought him still fit. Spending money to outfit a four-year-old for a funeral is one of the many bummers around the whole dying process.

The last time I saw my little brother he was running past me, full tilt, with a brownie in one hand and a Nanaimo bar in the other, yelling, "I love funerals!"

The people standing around me laughed at first, because this funeral is for my ninety-seven-year-old great-grand aunt who, by all accounts, lived a full life and had a great sense of humour, and would have been pleased as punch that a four-year-old was loving her funeral.

Then they stopped laughing when they remembered the funeral before this one was the four-year-old's mother's. My mother's.

Even though my mom also probably would have been pleased as punch that her small son was loving her funeral, people don't like to smile when they think of a forty-two-year-old woman's death.

I've spoken to the minister who performed the funeral service, and her husband, and the high school principal … honestly, I think I've spoken to half the residents of my Aunt Isabelle's small town. It feels weird that they're being so lovely and sympathetic to me when they're the ones who had daily contact with her; I hardly knew her. My mom's last visit here was with my biological father. He went out ice-fishing in the morning—leaving my heavily pregnant mother curled up in Aunt Isabelle's guest bed—and didn't come back at night.

That pre-natal visit was my one-and-only time in Perryside. A couple of times when I was younger Aunt Isabelle came to the city, but I only have vague memories of a lady wearing long, narrow skirts and neat cardigans. She gave me quarters, and figurines she saved from boxes of Red Rose tea. As soon as he was old enough not to choke on them, I passed the figurines on to Lief. He loves them, and I see them every day, lined up on his bedroom windowsill, but they don't give me any sense of the woman I'm here to mourn.

So, while I feel it should be me comforting the people who saw Aunt Isabelle every day, I'm not good at the comforting thing. I'm still deeply messed up when it comes to processing my mother's death. Instead, I ask questions about the town, and have learned more than I ever thought I would about the stone bridge in its centre. It's the oldest bridge in the province. It was designed by a Scotsman who came to live here nearly two hundred years ago.

I'm wondering if there's anything else in this town besides the bridge, when my stepdad taps my shoulder. "Lief is throwing up."

No surprise. Butter, laced with icing sugar, washed down with the fruit punch I saw him gulping earlier, mixed in with laps around the church hall, will do that.

Plus, the kid's just a natural-born puker.

"Where?" I ask.

Justin cocks his thumb toward a side hall. "In the bathroom. If you can go, I'll get the kit from the car."

"On my way."

The punch I've been clutching for some time is warm from my hands and that, combined with its orangey-pink colour, swirled with darker bits of pulp, means I'm not sad to set it down on the nearest windowsill before I head to the bathroom.

Lief's high-pitched voice tells me which of the small rooms he's in—"We already saw a kestrel and two hawks," he's saying. "Do you think I could see an owl?"— then his voice is cut off by a hiccupping wretching sound as his body rids itself of yet more high-octane dessert food.

Without the audio guidance, I would never have guessed my brother was in that particular bathroom because standing in the doorway is a very tall man in a dark suit. He crouches as Lief yaks and says, "You're OK buddy. Your dad will be back soon."

"I know!" Leif's voice is hollowed out by the acoustics of the toilet bowl. "I'll be fine. But I think Perry will be here first. My dad doesn't really like puke."

"Hi," I offer, and the crouching man whirls around so fast he loses his balance and nearly falls on his butt. He throws a foot out to steady himself and on his otherwise-shiny shoe I see something resembling my abandoned fruit punch, except chunkier. "Oh," I point at the shoe. "He got you."

"What?" He looks up at me, then his gaze follows my finger. "Oh, yeah. Just a bit, I guess." He shrugs. "It's OK. These shoes are really uncomfortable anyway. And they're at least one size too small." He's younger than I thought—probably close to my age—and I have the feeling these very shiny, very uncomfortable shoes might have been bought just for this funeral. It makes me feel even worse that my little brother barfed on them.

"Perry!" Lief raises his grinning face. "I made it to the toilet!"

"Mostly, anyway," I say. "Good job."

It's less the floating stomach contents in the bowl that put me off, and more the sight of Lief's chubby little hands gripping the rim, and the whole front of his body pressed against the porcelain. *Ugh. Public toilet germs. So, so gross.*

"Do you think you're done?" I ask. "Because then we could flush the toilet." *And scrub your hands ...*

I turn to thank the lanky presence in the doorway for keeping Lief company, but it's not him. It's my stepdad, eyes averted from the scene of the crime, holding out the Ziploc bag we keep in the trunk of the car for just such occasions. It contains an old facecloth, wipes, a spare t-shirt, a black garbage bag and anything else that might come in handy.

I squint at Lief and say, "You know, I think we can get away with just the facecloth today." I shrug off the light cardigan I'm wearing over my little black funeral dress, and do a swap with my stepdad—facecloth for cardigan—then turn on the hot water tap and snap my finger for Lief. "C'mere mister ..."

*   *   *

I look around my great-grand-aunt's kitchen and find nothing to do. Nothing immediate, anyway.

The Formica countertops are ancient but spotless. The mint green appliances gleam. The checkerboard kitchen floor is crumb- and dust-free.

Nothing like our kitchen at home where, at this time of night, I'd be washing half-a-million—or at least seventeen—small food containers needed for the three of us to take our various litterless lunches to work and school. Where flour, or breakfast cereal, or guinea pig food, would be sprinkled on the floor and I'd have to decide between sweeping it, or wiping the bottom of the stainless-steel fridge liberally peppered with Lief's small handprints.

I stare into the dark square of the window centred over the sink. Out there, I know, is the mowed area that slopes gently to the river—the river where the father I never knew died. The thought doesn't hurt me—honestly my fleeting thought about guinea pig food stings more with the death of Kiwi, our eight-year-old long-hair still fresh and raw.

Still, I can see why my mother never came back. Death: who wants to confront it?

With the kitchen light on, and no moon outside, the river could be lapping at the back doorstep and I wouldn't see it. I just see myself, seventeen years old and at loose ends with no household chores to do, and think it doesn't matter that my long hair could use a trim, or that if I was more skilled with make-up I wouldn't look so pale, because this is my social life. At today's funeral I spoke to at least a dozen people I've never met before, I noshed from a huge spread of food and drink, and I didn't get home until past my regular bedtime.

It's the biggest party I've been to in ages.

I listen to Justin's steps descending the narrow staircase and, sure enough, his also-pale face looms into view in the window beside mine.

"Hey," he says. "Why don't you go to bed?"

I turn to face him. "I feel like there's something I should be doing."

"That's just the point, Perry. There's nothing. Take a break, for once. Have a holiday. Get some sleep."

I lift one eyebrow. "A funeral holiday."

He smiles. "Never let it be said the Cochran-Archer family doesn't know how to vacation in style."

Most people I know at school complain about their step-parents. Most of them complain about their real parents, too. But what can I say about Justin Cochran except I know he's sad lots of the time, and I know he's usually tired, too, and he still tries his hardest to make Lief and me happy.

So, I push off the counter and say, "Well, those funeral festivities did wear me right out." And it's true; my hard-soled, pointy-toed shoes, with still not-enough wear in them to be broken in, are killing my feet. "I guess I'll head up and check on Lief and go to bed."

"Lief's fine," Justin says. "He's sound asleep. You don't have to worry about him."

"OK," I say.

I go upstairs and brush my teeth, and put on a tank top and stretchy shorts, and the last thing I do before climbing into bed is check on my little brother.

***

I swim my way up from a sucking sleep. I can't remember the last time I slept like this—deep and dreamless.

When I closed my eyes the clock said 10:32 p.m. and I wouldn't be shocked if it said 10:32 a.m. now—that's how long I feel like I've slept.

A couple of blinks tell me it's not quite that light outside my window, and a third blink informs me it's actually 7:32 a.m. Still, a good, long sleep.

The short trip to the bathroom past the open bedroom doors of Lief and my stepdad show me they're just as deep in sleep as I was a few minutes ago. Both are snoring. Lief's short snuffling breaths are sweet. Justin's are louder and they rattle. Now that I'm awake, I know they'll disturb me if I try to go back to bed.

Might as well run, then.

It's cooler here than in the city, and the bare skin up and down both my arms rises in goosebumps as soon as I step outside.

Maybe I should have brought something other than shorts and a tank top to run in. But I didn't, so there's just one way to push past the cold.

Run.

I have a decision to make at the end of the driveway. Right takes me past a couple of well-spaced neighbour's houses, and over a little causeway that marks the edge of town. I could run along Main Street, past the Tim Horton's where Justin fueled up before the funeral yesterday and where I stood in the women's washroom with my foot wedged against the door with its broken lock, listening to Lief tell me we might see a blue jay this weekend if we're lucky, and probably-almost-definitely we'll see wild turkeys.

Or, I can run the other way.

To … where?

The Road Not Taken.

I memorized it in grade two. I am someone with no indoor talents. I'm good at riding horses and running cross-country. So reciting a poem was all I could do for the school talent show, and the lines have stuck in my head ever since … "Two roads diverged in a wood and I, I took the one less traveled by, and that has made all the difference."

I turn left.

There is, almost immediately, forest. Which triggers a memory in my head. Justin saying something about Crown land. That, otherwise, the riverfront would be jammed with cottages. On the river side, then, uninterrupted forest. On the other side there's one driveway, but without a mailbox, just a municipal number—one of those ones that makes no attempt at charm or prettiness—glow-in-the-dark numbers on a metal plate.

When I exhale my breath steams into the morning light. My brain is still half full of sleep fog, which might be why the cold doesn't bother me. I'm not fully registering it.

There's another driveway ahead, and there's evidence of more effort here. There's a mailbox which—admittedly—has had a couple of run-ins with something bigger than it—maybe a snow plow?—but the dents have been painted over in a tasteful dark green. The municipal numbers are there, again. I'm pretty sure there must be some at Aunt Isabelle's place if I look more carefully, but they're clearly less important than a routered sign reading, **Riverhaven Farm.**

Much more interesting than the sign, though, is the fence I follow as I continue running past the driveway.

It's a classic split rail cedar fence. Not the fancy, straight-and-even, often white-painted or dark-stained type you see around the city, but the weathered, washed-grey, cedar wonders that zig-and-zag across the rough terrain, and that stay upright without benefit of nails, screws, or other hardware.

They're good fences for livestock, and my instinctive default is to hope this one contains horses.

I keep running, but I'm also peering into the trees.

Until ... *there* ...

Fuzzy shapes. They're mostly dark, and the trees behind them are near-black, but they shift and flow around a round-bale feeder and are clearly horses.

At least a dozen of them.

My run can pause. I push between two tree trunks—ignoring the twiggy branches that snag my hair and clothes—and lift my foot to the bottom rail of the fence. The horses are still quite a distance away, but it's clear they're nothing like the giraffe-like off-track-thoroughbred waiting for me at home. These are strong, stocky, with untrimmed legs, and ears, and manes either never, or rarely, pulled.

Happy and healthy, though. Curious. Friendly. One turns to me, his pricked ears outlined against a sliver of sky visible between the trees behind him. In the still morning air, his snort travels across the clearing.

Then he starts ambling. *Step, step, step*. There's a sway to his walk—an ease to his gait—and when he gets within reaching distance of my outstretched hands, he inserts his whiskery muzzle firmly into them.

"Oh, buddy, you're cute aren't you?"

I reach to straighten his forelock, and he's fine with that—not head-shy at all—in fact he presses the broad bone of his face against my fingers. *Scratch me. Right here.*

For a long minute he's happy with me rubbing his itchy forehead, then he exhales—if he was one of my friends standing around someone's locker at school, he'd complain, 'You guys are boring,'—and he wanders back to the not-very-exciting-but-at-least-edible contents of the round feeder.

I shiver as I watch his strong, square rump walk away. Standing still in this temperature—especially in a tank top, covered in a layer of drying sweat—is a bad idea.

I struggle back out to the road and launch back into my running rhythm.

Next time I'll have to bring a carrot. Then he'd stick around.

I shake my head. *Dummy.* It's Sunday. Lief and I have school tomorrow, and Justin has work. We have a few more hours here—that's all.

As I pass the tree-lined field on the return leg of my run I call out, "If I'd known you were here, I would have brought a carrot."

Just in case my shaggy friend is listening.

Chapter Two

The shower head's low, but the water pressure's good and the water's hot.

I bend my knees as I rinse the suds out of my hair and it works out fine.

The only shower is on the main floor, in the bathroom snugged between the kitchen and the side door.

I dove straight in after my run, hoping to avoid disturbing Justin and Lief asleep upstairs, but when I step out of the bathroom, hair wet around my shoulders, swaddled in a musty-smelling towel adorned with bright blue roses, Lief is roaring through the kitchen door. "Hey! Perry! I got a box of Timbits!" He swings the box high in the air and I pray for the cardboard handles to hold.

"Wow," I say. "Is that breakfast?"

Justin is right behind him. "No. This is breakfast." He plunks a bag reading **General Store** onto the counter and recites items as he lifts them out. "Bacon, baked beans, Red River bread, orange juice … oh, and eggs from Gil's place."

Lief nods hard and fast. "We were gonna go for a walk, but we saw Gil in town and he gave us a drive home, and gave us eggs, which were still warm …" Lief's eyes go wide as he says the words and he cups his hands under the Timbit box. I guess I'm supposed to imagine it's an egg.

"Who's Gil?" I ask.

"The neighbour down the road. You probably saw him at the funeral yesterday." Justin nods in the direction I didn't run this morning. "To be honest, it was a good thing we ran into him. I think I underestimated the walk to the store, and overestimated Mister's legs."

"Gil has a big truck!" Lief tells me. "I sat in the middle, and it's red, and …"

"Let your sister go get dressed for breakfast," Justin says. "You can tell her all about it while we have bacon and eggs."

Upstairs, as I shrug into stretchy pants and a soft hoodie I smile at the image of Lief sandwiched between Justin and some old dude, in his old truck, with my brother thinking it's the best thing ever.

Maybe Justin was right, after all. Between my great night's sleep, and my morning run, and Lief's adventures on Main Street, maybe this has been a little holiday for us. A Cochran-Archer vacation.

It just shows, despite my best friend Sata's complaints, I can leave home. I did leave home. Next time she has a go at me I'll have this to throw back in her face. I went four-hundred kilometres from home and I'm just fine, thank you very much.

I look around the room. It's narrow; containing a three-quarter sized bed with an iron bedstead that would look hokey in our renovated house in the city, but fits just perfectly under the low-sloping ceiling here. The floors are some kind of wide-planked wood that don't match the floors anywhere else in the house, and the closet is so shallow you have to turn the hangers on an angle to be able to shut the door.

The window, though ... set into the dormer, it's higher than it could be otherwise. The old glass has a waviness to it that blurs the edges of the yellows, oranges, and reds of the maples outside, so the trees look like balls of late-season fire. There's land visible across the river. It's Quebec. A whole other province so close it looks like you could swim to it. Except for the currents, Justin's warned both Lief and me—never trust a river. Ultimately, it was the currents that killed my father—eating away at the ice he thought he could trust.

Justin knows because he grew up here, too—was a senior on the boys high school basketball team when my father was a junior. He came home from med school in the city to attend my father's funeral, and my eight-month pregnant mother asked him to drive her back—

getting into the passenger seat of Justin's SUV and leaving behind her car and any ties she had to this place.

Justin's been in our lives ever since—first occasionally, and casually, then officially and constantly—and he was the one who used to come back here twice a year and help Aunt Isabelle with the big spring and fall chores she couldn't do on her own.

He knows this house, and this town, and that river—the good and the bad of all of them.

I wonder if my mom ever stood at this window, gazing out to the province across the river.

I try, but I can't picture it.

The failure rouses the first faint feeling of panic in me. It's fine, I tell myself. It's normal. You never knew her here. You'll be home soon.

I take one deep breath. Then another. I don't hyperventilate, or cry, or run screaming downstairs telling Justin we have to leave right now, right this second.

However, I do think maybe I won't be bragging to Sata about my trip after all.

***

"Storm windows!" Justin says as I stack our breakfast plates, then layer the cutlery on top of them.

"Say, what?" I set the dirty dishes down on the counter by the dishwasher and tug at the door. It doesn't open.

"Storm windows. We have to put them on today." He's swiping at the front of Lief's shirt with a damp cloth.

"If I knew what you were talking about I'd know what you mean." I have the plates scraped, with all the scraps on a napkin, but I still haven't managed to open the dishwasher.

"How can you not know what storm windows are?" While Justin's turned to me, Lief wriggles out of his chair.

"How can you not know what a martingale is?" I counter. Justin still doesn't understand the difference between a horse and a pony, so I know I've got him there.

Lief claps his hands. "Storm windows are outside windows that cover the inside windows!" Justin and I both stare at him. "What?" he asks. "Gil told me."

I give another tug on the front of the dishwasher and, this time, the whole thing lurches forward. For a second, I think I've yanked the unit out of the wall. Then I realize it's actually a huge internal basket that's slid out. "What the ...?"

There's a twitch behind Justin's smile that tells me he's trying not to laugh out loud. "It's a dishwasher—maybe you've heard of them?"

I peer into the depths of the drawer in front of me. "Am I supposed to climb inside to load it?" I shake my head. "Forget it. Cancel that question. Go outside and start working on your gale windows ..."

"Storm!" Lief interrupts.

I stick my tongue out at him. "Storm. Whatever. I'll be out after I figure out how to get the dishes in here without breaking them."

As the door closes behind them I mutter, "Storm windows. Ancient dishwashers." I hold up the mug Justin used for his coffee. It's a kind of translucent milky colour, with a band of olive green flowers running just below the rim. It clashes badly with the mint green appliances. "This place is a time warp."

Then I bend almost double at the waist to settle an equally ugly cereal bowl in the bottom of the dishwasher.

Chapter Three

When I make it outside, there's a row of wood-framed windows leaned against the bottom half of the house, and nobody in sight.

Upon closer inspection, the frames are white with bits of the paint just beginning to flake—note to self: do *not* be around at re-painting time—and the glass is just as wavy as in the bedroom upstairs. If Lief is right, that one of these is being put over that window, it'll distort the view so badly it will make it nearly impossible to see across the river.

A giggle—Lief's giggle—drifts to my ears, and I go looking for him.

He's at the edge of the lawn, where the trees start and he's laughing and saying, "No-no-no!" to the guy from yesterday. It takes me a minute to recognize him, because the shoes he's wearing have no puke on them, and I'm pretty sure they're steel-toed.

Today he's wearing jeans and a plaid lumberjack shirt along with his work boots. Today he looks even younger than yesterday.

Just right for me … the thought flits into one side of my mind and I push it just as fast out the other side. Because I am boring. I am damaged goods. I am No. Fun. At. All. I know because the guy who came very close to being my boyfriend—Adam Penske—told me so in the weeks that followed my mom's death when I developed the habit of staying home and folding laundry, and reading Lief stacks of bedtime stories instead of … well, to be honest, instead of doing anything else at all.

Other than making time to see North. But North's non-negotiable.

The young, cute guy who is none of my concern, is pointing into the forest, saying, "What are you talking about? Look—that's an owl!" and Lief's sputtering, "A *plas-tic* owl, silly!"

I squint through the trees and manage to make out one of those ugly owls people use to scare pigeons, wedged between the trunk and one of the branches of a big maple. Lief's right—plastic.

"Oh, wow," the guy shakes his head. "I can't believe you said that. That's Hootie and he *hates* being called plastic."

Lief smacks his forehead and stamps his foot. "But he *is* plastic!"

There's a hooting noise and—to be fair to the guy— even if it doesn't sound natural, it also doesn't sound like he made it. He seems to be able to throw his voice.

"What was that?" Lief asks.

"That was Hootie. He says he's glad to meet you, but he wishes you would say he's *resin*."

"Resin!" Lief's laughing again, then he drops his voice. "Wait ... look, there's a cardinal!"

"Hey!" Justin's voice carries across the lawn. "Where did my helpers go?"

Lief runs toward his dad's voice, saying, "Dad! You scared the cardinal away. Gil was pretending to show me an owl, but it wasn't a real owl ..."

Gil ... "Oh, *you're* Gil." Wow, my picture of Gil was way off—like a trillion degrees of adorableness off. If I didn't live several hundred remote and rural kilometres away from this guy, his ridiculously high cheekbones, combined with absurdly long eyelashes would definitely tempt me to slot a coffee-shop rendezvous into my schedule.

He nods, and says, "And you are the frequently mentioned Perry. Does that mean you'll be moving here?"

"Pardon me?"

"Well you're named after this place, right? Perryside? Seems like this spot is ready-made for you."

My chest tightens. Then a strange recklessness floods me, and for a fleeting second I'm tempted to tell him the truth. To admit to someone I've never met before that I can never, ever leave my neighbourhood, my street, my house. That those are the only places I still feel my mom. Still remember her. That sometimes I leave school at lunch just so I can go home and sit in the kitchen and squint my eyes and imagine she's there, washing dishes, talking to me.

To tell him I'm only here this weekend because I knew it was important to Justin, and also because the city's replacing the water mains on our street and there's no water at our house right now anyway.

I bite the inside of my cheek. There's no way I'm telling a complete stranger any of that. I walk after Lief so I won't have to meet Gil's eyes. It lets me just laugh and say, "If you knew more about my last twenty-four hours, you'd never say I belong here. I brought clothes for the wrong season, I can't figure out how anything works in this house, and I don't even know what blizzard windows are."

His forehead wrinkles. "Storm windows?"

I snap my fingers. "Yeah, that's it: *storm* windows. I'm pretty sure I could get run out of Perryside for not knowing what they are."

We've reached the stack leaning against the foundation of the house. Gil touches one. "Well, this is a storm window. It's an ..."

"... outside window that covers an inside window," I say.

"See? You know what a storm window is."

"That was a direct quote from my four-year-old brother who, I think, learned it from you."

Gil shrugs. "Hey, as long as you learned it, it doesn't really matter how you learned it. There's hope for you yet."

"Hope, how?" Justin's coming around the corner of the house carrying yet another storm window, with Lief gripping the corner—more being dragged along with it, than carrying it.

Gil steps forward and lifts the storm window out of their hands. "I think Perry's just about earned her storm window certification."

Justin swipes his hand across his forehead, leaving a smudgy streak. "Well, that's amazing news, because I'm not sure how such a small house can have so many windows." He looks at me, and hooks his thumb back toward the shed. "The rest are in there."

I look at Gil. "Thank you very much for that."

He grins. "Consider me the Perryside welcoming committee. At your service."

A service I don't need. But, hey, I don't have to get into that with him. I'll never see him again after today.

* * *

We haven't even hit the outskirts of town yet—we're stopped at the single traffic light on Main Street—and

• 23 •

Lief's already conked out in his booster seat, arms flung wide, mouth hanging open.

Justin looks in the rear-view mirror. "Hard to believe that's the same kid who didn't sleep for most of the first year of his life."

I remember Lief not sleeping. I remember Justin slipping him into a baby carrier and taking him out for long walks through the neighbourhood just as I was heading up to bed. I remember sometimes I'd hear Lief, early in the morning, and I'd scoop him out of his crib and take him downstairs to watch old Mighty Machines DVDs so Justin and my mom could get an extra hour of sleep.

I can't remember my mom at all. I know she was tired. I know she put her car keys in the fridge, and left the phone in the microwave. If I was home I could stand in the kitchen and picture her doing those things. But right now, so far away, I can't at all. Her image escapes me. The panic bubbles and I bite my lip and try not to sniff too loudly.

"Hey ..." The light turns green and once Justin's put the car in gear and pulled forward he taps my leg. "It's OK. I feel it too."

"You do?" I look at him more closely. His eyes are a bit shinier than usual.

He nods. "I always find it hard to leave here. I had a great weekend with you and Lief. But, don't worry, we can come back another time."

I suck in my breath. I'm definitely not going to tell him I'm counting the kilometres between here and our front door in the city. "Um. Yeah. Another time." Like sometime way, way in the future.

Just not anytime soon.

As the kilometres roll away under us with each one taking us closer to home, the lulling combination of the autumn sun slanting through the car windows, and the hum of the tires on the highway make my eyelids so, so heavy.

I'm trying not to let them shut, because I know I won't be able to pry them open again and it seems unfair to leave Justin to tackle the long drive alone.

Besides, it's pretty. We spin by lake, after lake, after sun-sparkled lake, broken only by long stands of mostly coniferous trees. Sun, water, and greenery. No intrusions by gas stations or coffee shops.

It's so different from home, and it'll be my last trip for a long time so I really should get it stored away in my memory ... but I'm seriously wiped. My head falls forward and I jerk it back again.

"Hey." The tiny edge of gravel in Justin's voice comes across as softly soothing. Everything feels like a lullaby right now.

I struggle to sit straighter. "Yeah? Do you want me to check the route?"

"I want you to go to sleep."

I glance in the back where Lief is breathing deep and evenly, making twitching ticks with the thumb and fingers on his left hand.

"He's tired. He's sleeping. You're tired. You should sleep."

"What about you?" I ask.

"I'm fine. If I get tired, I'll pull over. Simple as that."

"But ..." But. But my eyes are grainy, and the sun is warming my skin and turning my brain to mush, and ...

... *blink, blink, blink.* The car's slowing down. Justin must be pulling over for a break. The tires don't hum anymore, instead they roll, gravel crunching below us.

The light that sweeps over my eyelids is bright but without warmth. What's going on? Eyes open. It's dark—night—and that light was from a light standard. A very familiar one; the one at the end of North's barn's driveway.

"What ...?" I squint at Justin.

He smiles. "Hey, sleepyhead." Then continues. "I figured you'd like to check in on the big guy."

Um ... yes. "Wow, thanks. Do we have time?"

"It'll have to be a quick—" He's still saying "—visit," and I'm already pushing the car door open, stepping into the inky cool-tinged night air, taking unsteady steps while a tingle of pins and needles drains from my car-cramped legs.

Everything about being here feels wrong. The gravel is sharp under the thin soles of my ballet flats. My loose hair falls in my face. My arm, reaching for the barn door, is draped with a fuzzy sweater—a horse-hair-and-shavings magnet.

But ... would I rather skip seeing North? No.

I'll just have to be extra careful to keep my vulnerable toes away from his hard hooves.

The barn is Sunday-night quiet. At least I assume this lack of activity is normal for a Sunday night because I, myself, can't remember ever being here at this time on a Sunday.

It's perfect because when I say, "Hey buddy!" there's no chatter of other riders, or whisking of a broom, or horseshoes ringing on the barn floor, to mask my voice, and when a rustle comes from a stall halfway down the aisle, there are no noises to cover that sound, either.

When I get to his stall, North has his face pressed against the door.

"Hello," I say, and his ears pitch so far forward they nearly touch at the tips. "Now, whoa."

I slide the door to the side and, even though he doesn't want to, North waits. I said "whoa" and he knows what "whoa," means.

I back away, until I'm standing right between a set of cross-ties, and say, "OK, come on," and my lanky grey boy surges out of his stall, takes the half-dozen steps he needs to reach me, then stops, head low, so I can scratch his poll, and straighten his forelock, and tell him what a good horse he is.

I'm circling his itchy spot with the jelly scrubber, and he's stretching his head out, cocked sideways, lips flapping, when the barn door creaks open and Lief comes flying in, closely followed by Justin.

Lief throws himself at me, yelling, "Hey Perry! Hey North!" and North barely twitches an ear in his direction. The Small One doesn't scare North. In fact, The Small One often brings carrots, so North—who is quite picky about his people—tolerates him.

"Sorry," Justin says. "Pent-up energy after a four-hour drive."

"C'n I give him a carrot?" Lief asks.

"Of course. There are a few left in the bag in my tack locker."

Lief scampers off to find a carrot, and I continue North's grooming, and Justin grabs a broom to sweep up the clods of dirt I picked out of North's hooves and there's a second, right before we leave, when I unsnap the cross ties from North's halter, and he lowers his head to huff warm air through Lief's little-boy-downy hair, and Lief lets out one of those burbling, infectious, little-kid giggles that make your insides float and your whole face smile, and Justin and I look at him, then look at each other, looking at him, and in that second we are a family.

Not just any family, but the most perfectly, whole, healthy, happy family in all of Canada—or maybe the world—then *Mom*, I think, and a wave of guilt swamps me because, there I go, forgetting her, and it's even worse because North was her horse, and I wouldn't even have him if it wasn't for her.

It just shows it's time to get home to where it's easier to remember her.

North catches a lock of Lief's hair between his lips, and Lief squeals. North's ears sweep back, Justin swoops Lief out of the way, and I snap my fingers to put North's focus back on me and say, "Good times are over, big guy. Back to your stall."

Chapter Four

Fall rain, cold and steady. By the time I get to school the puddles have infiltrated the seam at the sole of my shoes. I'll have wet socks all day.

I throw back my shoulders as a single rivulet of icy water snakes its way from my collar down my back.

Splash, splash, splash through rainwater collected in the depressions of the worn stone steps, and push through the hulking double doors into the steamy boiler-driven heat of the school.

Our school is heritage if you're on the neighbourhood association and determined to overturn a proposal to have it torn down for a new build. It's out-of-date and inaccessible if you're a council member fighting for that new build. If you're a student—especially a grade nine—it's rambling, and confusing, and intimidating. Three storeys—or four, or five—of crumbling brick tacked together in a succession of additions since 1917, none of it designed for people in wheelchairs, or with broken legs, or just trying to feel at home in a new school.

I'm not a grade nine. In fact, this is my last year here, so I go on auto-pilot. Climb the first staircase as I loosen my scarf. Step over outstretched legs of students leaning against their lockers in the math wing. Up a half-flight of stairs and down the other side while I unbutton my coat. Around the corner and up another set of stairs, trying not to drop anything as I transfer all my outdoor gear to my arm.

"Perry! Hey, wait up!"

Sata makes me smile. Sata makes everyone smile. There's nobody with eyes as deep, and lively, and velvety-brown as Sata. The only beach we live anywhere near is halfway across a very busy city, on a freshwater lake, but Sata's long, black hair sports beach waves every day of the year, and still manages to shine. So, she's striking, yes, but also smart, and funny. I hit the jackpot when Sata and I became best friends in grade school, and it shows how loyal she is that she still treats me like her bestie even though I've done nothing at all to reciprocate her friendship since before my mom died.

I nod toward the classroom she just left. "How was Model UN?" Sata and I have been in MUN together since grade nine. We were supposed to co-chair this year, until I said, "I really can't. Justin needs me to take Lief to daycare now."

The truth is, I *sometimes* take Lief to daycare, and that's because I volunteered. Justin would hate to think I'm passing up school activities to help out at home. "I want you to be happy," he always says.

"The Bellwood conference is coming up. You should come and win Best Delegate for the fourth straight year."

I know Sata's offering because she also wants me to be happy. What I can't explain to Justin or Sata is I'm doing what makes me happy this year. I'm filled with FOMO, but it takes an entirely different form than with most other people. I have a massive fear of missing out on an important milestone in Lief's life, or of the three of us not having the sit-down dinners that were so important to my mom.

I need to preserve our home. I need to hold onto my mom's memory. That's what makes me happy these days.

As we climb the final stairwell to our lockers, Sata asks, "How was the funeral?"

It was good.

It's the first thought into my head. Which ... is just wrong. You can't say that about a funeral, can you? Plus, I hate being away from home. It stresses me out.

Except ... it didn't this past weekend. At least, for a lot of the time it didn't. Which fills me with a weird feeling of confusion, or guilt, or something I don't really want to feel right now, so instead I say, "Lief ate pounds of baking, then puked it all up, Justin fried freshly laid eggs for breakfast, and it was so quiet we all slept in."

The warning chimes go—*bing, bing, bong*—and Sata and I pick up our pace toward our lockers. "Maybe we can go out soon, for a smoothie or something, and you can tell me more about it?" She looks happy and hopeful.

I smile. "Yeah. Maybe." And, in that moment, it's possible I mean it. At least a little bit.

***

"Home. What is it?" Mr. Tidwell taps the whiteboard where he's all-capped *HOME* in black dry-erase marker.

There are two Geography teachers. Mr. Knight is old school—memorize the place names of one hundred Canadian communities with a population smaller than five thousand. If you can do that, and spell them correctly, you can get a hundred per-cent on the final exam.

Then there's Mr. Tidwell. "This will be the topic of your summative for this course," he says. "Home. How can we identify and define the concept of home and its meaning from a geographic perspective?"

"Dumb," Cody Heller mouth breathes behind me.

"Huh?" Annette Holleran scrunches up her nose and rubs her forehead. "I don't understand."

"Interesting." Rosemary Cranbrooke, perpetual winner of our grade's Academic Achievement award has already block printed *HOME* in her impeccable penmanship, using her refillable fountain pen in her Moleskin notebook.

And me? My stomach does an unexpected, slo-mo, flip. I flatten my hand against my waistband. The tuna I had for lunch? I'm pretty sure it was fine ...

"Let's start simply," Mr. Tidwell says. "Answer quickly—don't overthink it—what is home?" He scans the classroom. "Rosemary?"

"A place of residence." She's so confident she doesn't even lift her answer at the end with an implied question mark.

"Well ... yes ... but I was hoping for a less rigid definition. Annette?"

Annette blinks twice. "Um, where I go after school?"

"Sure. Good. Cody?"

Cody lifts his head from the desktop where he's been sprawled as though it's a huge effort. "Where you hang your hat?" He looks around, grinning, and the members of his posse who are in this class with us, snicker.

"Home is wherever you are, sir!" somebody else yells.

"No, home is where the refrigerator is full." "Where my laundry gets done." "Where I can charge my phone."

One girl, holding onto rules in the face of all this exuberant anarchy, holds her hand up. "Yes? Zara?"

Her cheeks go slightly red, and she says, "I guess home is probably where your parents are."

"Good! Yes!" Mr. Tidwell is rubbing his hands together and turning to the board, marker in hand, to capture the results of our brainstorming session.

Meanwhile, my stomach is doing a complete flop back the other direction, and I know it's not from the tuna.

The thing is, I agree with Zara.

Which is a problem, because my mom's not at home anymore.

But lots of bits of her are.

The indentations made by the wheels of the hospital bed still mark the area rug from when she got too sick to go up the stairs and we converted the living room to a bedroom.

I still expect to see pill bottles lining the windowsill every time I lower the blinds.

And those are just the most recent things.

There's the quilt on my bed she made from my baby clothes she couldn't bear to get rid of.

The set of furniture in Lief's room I helped her sand and re-paint in the months before he was born.

The microwave that always boiled the milk over when she used it to make hot chocolate ... then she'd turn and throw her arms up in the air, and say, "Plus, the milk's not even hot!" She hated that microwave.

There's ... well there's something in every room.

For me home is the place I lock myself into to hold onto the essence of my dead mother.

I don't think I'll be saying that for my summative, though.

***

Cute new barista at the juice bar. Sata texts me.

I eye the macaroni and cheese left in the corner of the Pyrex dish. Big Tupperware or small Tupperware?

My phone buzzes again. **As in the juice bar around the corner. Like fifty steps from your front door. You could tell me about your weekend over a Heavenly Huckleberry.**

"Perry! Perry!" Lief's high-pitched voice floats down the stairs.

I snap the container lid into place—*come on, close, don't ooze*—then scoot to the bottom of the stairs. "What is it?"

"Lief," Justin's voice breaks in. "I'm right here; you can ask me. Perry's busy."

Lief answers, "But Mama's missing!"

Mama Monkey is the stuffed animal Lief can*not* sleep without. Mama Monkey goes missing several times a week. I'm very accustomed to looking for Mama Monkey. I call up the stairs. "Justin? Do you know where Mama is?"

"Sorry," he says.

My phone vibrates again. **Seriously, Perry. He looks like Dev Patel. He's giving me free smoothies now. He has a brother. You need to come.**

Sorry. No can do. Small emergency with Lief. Have a smoothie for me.

I power the phone off and drop it on the hall table. "Coming!" I say, and skip every second step on my way upstairs.

***

Lief is lying back in the tub, a ruff of bubbles around his neck. I kneel in the doorway, sorting socks, folding underwear; trying to tame the tsunami of laundry that seemed to explode out of our bags when we got back from the funeral in Perryside.

Not minding, because it keeps me busy.

The air is steamy warm. The underfloor heating radiates toasty comfort through the tiles under my knees. Lief half-sings, half-babbles and I listen to his sing-songy tone without really paying attention to his words—"Alice the camel has seven humps ..." is interrupted with, "No, no, no William! I was using those scissors," followed closely by, "Lavender blue, dilly, dilly ..."

Lief's day, spilled out in a way that shows he's normal, happy, nobody's bullying him—all is good.

"... Mama ..." he says.

I look up. "Yes, don't worry. I found her. She's waiting on your pillow."

He's not listening to me, though. His eyes have a soft-focus quality, and they're gazing somewhere behind me and higher up.

"Hi, Mama," he says, and the way his whole face lifts sends a quivering flutter right through my core.

It's happening again.

Lief's eyes flick to me for a brief second. "Mama's here, Perry."

My little brother is always angelic to look at—perfect in every way from his unblemished skin, to his crazy-long lashes, and the adorableness of his little ears and nose—but in these moments he glows.

I hold my breath. I sit perfectly still. I want this to last as long as it can. I don't want to be the one who ends it.

Then Lief blinks twice, drops his gaze back to the bubbles, lifts two heaping palmfuls up in front of his eyes, and asks, "Did you really find Mama Monkey?"

Aanndd ... we're back.

"I, uh, yeah, I did."

"Where was she?"

"She was smunched between your headboard and the wall."

Lief giggles. "Smunched?"

I arrange the folded clothes in a careful pile against the wall right outside the bathroom and, fighting a rush of pins and needles to my lower legs, stumble to my feet. "Well, she might have been mooshed."

"Are you going to moosh me in my towel?" he asks.

"I don't know—I might scrumple you."

***

I'm sitting at the kitchen island, holding a highlighter, running my eyes across the summative hand-out Mr. Tidwell gave us, with not one single word highlighted.

There's a long-since cooled mug of hot chocolate off to the left. If I look at the way the brown milk has congealed around the marshmallow, I'll never drink hot chocolate again.

Justin clomps up the stairs from the basement, t-shirt dark with sweat from his evening workout on his bike trainer. "What's up?"

I shake my head. "I have to start my geography summative and I'm kind of drifting aimlessly."

"Can I see?" he asks.

I push the paper toward him and he reads out loud: "How can we identify and define the concept of home and its meaning from a geographic perspective? What is home to you, and why?" He blinks twice, fast. His mouth twitches.

"What?" I ask.

Now he shakes his head. "No. Nothing. It's an interesting assignment."

"And one I'm struggling with."

"What did he say when he assigned it?"

"He said not to overthink it."

Justin nods. "Yeah. I guess I would have said, 'Just be honest.' Same kind of thing."

Easier said than done. Honesty would be, *"Home is the house where I hang on to my mother's spirit."* I'm not brave enough to be that honest.

My gaze falls on a picture stuck to our fridge.

This one is two-thirds North's grey muzzle and whiskers, with my face cut-off in the background. Not a good photo, but one that makes me smile. "Home is where my horse is?"

Justin snaps his fingers. "That's honest."

OK. I can write that. It'll work. It'll even be unique. I can sense an A+ idea when one jumps into my head.

"Speaking of honesty ..." Justin says. "This hot chocolate is honestly the most disgusting thing I've seen all week."

"I know. I'm trying to pretend it's not there."

"Go to bed, I'll take care of it."

"You'd do that?"

"I owe you for finding the monkey."

Justin reaches for the mug, and I don't hang around. I'm not about to be here if he changes his mind. And now that I know how valuable the information is, I'm also not about to ever show him Mama Monkey's hiding places.

Chapter Five

The bell rings at 1:40. By 1:41 I have my locker open. At 1:43 I'm pushing through the doors into a sunny September afternoon arched over with the clear, searingly blue sky that only comes in the fall when the night frosts blow away the summer's haze and humidity.

1:55 sees me backing out of our driveway.

As much as I'm counting the minutes, and as badly as I want to get to North, I take the long way to the highway, because the short way takes me by the hospital. The one where my mom died.

I don't want to think of her there. Want to keep her memories sacred in our house, so I spend five extra minutes, and take the longer route to the highway, and I still almost always get to the barn by 2:30, so that's all fine anyway.

I walk into shavings scattered over the texturized rubber floor, a wheelbarrow skewed in front of a stall, dust motes floating in the light from the doors open at each end of the aisle.

Heaven. Home.

It's because I have this that I've never felt a need to have a huge posse of friends at school. It's because I have this that it's easier than it should be to distance myself from my best friend.

A forkful of shavings sails out of the open stall door and into the barrow and a voice calls, "That you Perry?"

"None other."

"Must be Day Two—did I get that right?"

Karen appears in the doorway. A near-foot shorter than me, there's no way she weighs a hundred pounds, but she considers carrying less than two hay bales a waste of time, and there's a 17.2hh Clyde cross at the barn who can only be loaded in the trailer by Karen.

The first afternoon I showed up at the barn at 2:30 Karen pulled the bulky phone receiver she always totes around out of her back pocket and asked, "Do I need to call your dad?" I had to show her my timetable—thankfully, I had a copy in my car—and explain this year I have a spare which alternates. On Day One, it's the first period after lunch, but on Day Two, it's my last period of the day. So I can leave. So I can come here.

"I'm not skipping school!" I'd said.

"You'd better not be—I did, and look at me now."

"You work with horses all day!" I'd protested.

She shook her head. "There are better things in store for you Perry Archer. You stay in school."

Even if she believes me now, I know better than to ever skip school to come to the barn. Karen might play dumb, but if I ever showed up early on a Day One, she'd be on the phone to Justin in no time.

"Well," she says now. "The big guy will be happy to see you. He's himself. Had a good gallop around the paddock. Showed one of the new geldings who was boss. Pretty sure Clara has a couple she'd like exercised if you're so inclined."

"She in the office?"

"Lunging in the sand ring."

"'Kay. Thanks. Later."

I continue to the far doors and step out into sunshine that can only feel this good in the fall, when lingering moments of warmth become precious.

Clara doesn't even turn to me when I lean on the fence, but the wildly swiveling ears of the mare she's lunging mean she knows I'm here. The mare's narrow and finely built, with a bit too much hip bone jutting out; one or two more ribs showing than would be ideal. Her lunge circle wobbles. As I watch, her nostrils flare and she swings her hindquarters off the track and dances sideways.

"I think she'd do better under saddle. Go grab some tack. Jessie's should fit."

There's no hi-how-are-you. Or, rather, there is, and this is it. "Ride a horse for me?" "OK." It's the best greeting I can imagine.

Without wasting any time, I go to hunt out Jessie's tack.

***

My time with North comes after I've scrambled up on the skinny mare's wobbly back and tried to give her a bit of confidence that a rider is a good thing. *Your rider can help you. Your rider will take care of you.*

Between the mare and North, I give a very different ride—and message—to a stocky, stubborn wall-eyed piebald school pony. *Your rider is the boss. You cannot rub your rider off on the fence. Your rider decides when you canter and what you jump.*

With Clara satisfied—"that should hold him ... until the message wears off and it doesn't anymore,"—I shove a carrot in my back pocket and head to my horse's paddock.

You wouldn't know North is twenty-five. He doesn't know he's twenty-five.

Old age has probably added white hairs to the sculpted lines of his face but, as a light—nearly white—grey it's impossible to tell.

He's still tall, still lean; and from the pictures I've seen, still looks not too much different from the day he came off the racetrack twenty years ago.

Back when my mother bought him. Back before she knew her high-school-sweetheart-turned husband would fall through the ice in their hometown. Before she knew she'd have me, and I'd love horses, too. Before she knew cancer would hit her so hard she wouldn't be able to make it to the barn anymore and her horse would become mine.

North nickers when I call him and meets me at the paddock gate. His two turn-out mates are young and compliant, and North's biting teeth and flying hooves have taught them a few basic rules. *Don't wander anywhere near North's pile of hay. Stay ten feet back from the gate when I come to catch him. North's carrots are sacred.*

I close the gate behind my horse and the other two press forward. With North snatching mouthfuls of the long, green grass outside the paddock, it's now OK for them to take carrots from me. The bay gelding reaches for his treat, and the chestnut filly bares her teeth at him. There's always a pecking order to be established.

North strides beside me with his proud, swinging walk. He carries his head and tail high.

I secure the sand ring gate behind us, let him go, and he breaks into a trot. Which is when the problem with North becomes evident.

He's dead lame.

After years of vet, chiropractor, and massage therapy consultations, after building him up on a soundness program from hand-walking, through walk and into careful trot and canter work three separate times, only to have him one day go right back to horrific limping, after trying medication, food, and corrective shoes, I've accepted it. North is lame, and North is old; North will be lame for the rest of his life.

He swoops by me, shaking his head, prancing in a dance that would be gorgeous if it wasn't for the short step every time his off hind hits the ground.

North is a perfectly healthy, highly energetic thoroughbred, born to move—and move fast—who excelled in his second career as a prelim-level eventer, and now I don't ride him at anything faster than a walk, and I'm not even sure if I should be doing that.

The challenge is to keep him occupied. To make his brain work so he won't kick his stall apart or try to jump out of his paddock.

So we play.

I run from one end of the ring, to the other and he follows in his forward, broken trot. We play tag; not with any set rules, just with lots of moving and interaction.

We get in a good half-hour before Clara's afternoon group of moms-who-ride start leading their horses out of the barn, then I take North in and groom him ears to tail, and while I'm doing that a small girl arrives—the first of Clara's next lesson group, and one who's a particular fan of North.

She stands off to the side while I pick out his hooves and, when I straighten, asks, "May I?"

I laugh. "He won't be very happy if you don't."

North knows the girl has a carrot in her back pocket and he knows it's for him. That quiet confidence gives him the patience to wait politely, but if she goes away without handing over the treat, I'll see ears pinned back, a whisk of the tail, a stamp of the hoof.

She steps forward and palms him her carrot. "He looks so beautiful," she says as North crunches her offering, and she strokes his nose.

Which—I step back and tilt my head sideways and squint my eyes—she's right. He does. He looks really, really great.

Only a couple of his usually prominent ribs show. The late afternoon sun highlights the shine in his coat, and his mane and tail are thick and full.

North is by no means an easy keeper, and there was a period when we were playing musical barns with him. The stable where he was settled and happy closed, and the place we moved him to switched his stall and his paddock almost every week. That was when his hair started falling out in clumps. The barn after that was next-door to a dog breeding and boarding facility where dogs barked all day and North ran the fence lines and dropped weight at an alarming rate.

And then his original stable—this place—re-opened; this time run by the daughter of the woman who had retired and closed it. My mother made sure North was the very first boarder back through the double barn doors and my happy, healthy horse tells me it was the right decision.

As I take him back to turn him out, I scratch his shoulder. "I guess we know where your home is, huh?"

He lifts his head and snorts, then sends a ringing whinny toward his paddock, warning the two youngsters crowded by the gate that he's on his way back.

Chapter Six

I've just come back from a before-school run, when I hit the traffic jam at the side door. I'm coming in, and Lief and Justin are heading out, and the landing at the top of the basement stairs is nowhere near big enough for the three of us.

Lief plunks himself right down in the middle of it because when you're four, and you need to put your boots on, everybody else had better get out of your way.

Justin steps around Lief, hugging the wall, and I take a wide step over the yawn of the basement stairs, and that way we each end up where we need to be—me going inside for breakfast and a shower, Justin dropping Lief off at before-school care on his way to work.

"Anything up today?" Justin asks. It's his touchstone question—it bookends my days. *Anything up today?* in the morning, and *Anything happen today?* in the evening.

I don't tell him everything, but I usually try to at least tell him something. He's a pretty easy audience.

"I have my long lunch today so I might go to the library to return those books ..."

"Oh, those books ... I'm sorry."

Justin doesn't have many vices, but he does like to check books out of the library with Lief, then not return them. I can vividly picture my mom standing right here, shouldering a canvas tote sold as a library fundraiser that said **This bag has a story**, bulging with the hard edges and pointy corners of dozens of books. "Did I tell you I had to pay off forty-seven dollars in fines to be allowed to renew Lief's library card? And that's with a five-dollar limit for fines on kids' materials."

The memory's so vivid that for just a second it's like she's actually here. My heart lifts, as do the corners of my mouth. If I'm lucky I can ride this shot of happiness through most of my day.

"Oh! Oh! Oh! Do I get a lollipop?" The children's librarian gives out lollipops for each twenty-five books checked out on a child's library card. Justin's fines alone probably keep her in lollipops for a year. Lief looks like a dog chasing his tail as he turns in circles trying to shrug his arm through the left strap of his backpack. "Do I, Perry?"

I'm afraid he's going to spin himself right down the basement stairs. "I'll ask, Liefy." I grab the strap on the top of his backpack, and while I hold him still, he manages to slip his arm into place.

"Thanks Perry! Bye Perry!" Lief calls, and Justin sends me a quick wave, and with a creak of the door hinges, and a rattle of the loose pane of glass in the window, punctuated by the cloud of cold air that swirls around my ankles, they're gone and I'm alone in a house where the only sounds are the humming of the fridge compressor and the background whoosh of the furnace.

I love Lief, but there's something nice about filling my bowl so full the cereal spills over onto the counter and settling down to eat it with nothing but my own thoughts to keep me company.

Just as I'm finishing, and wondering if I should pour myself another bowl, my phone buzzes.

It'll be Sata answering my **Hey, wanna come to the library with me at lunch?** text. I know she'll say yes as long as we can drop into the vintage clothing store on the block next to the library. It's my way of making up for ditching her at the smoothie place.

It's not Sata. It takes me several seconds to figure out who it is, because it comes in as an unrecognized number, with an area code nowhere near here, and the message consists of a big, black bird with an iridescent sheen to its plumage and thick foliage behind it. Half my brain thinks there's something familiar about the background, then the other half says, *Um yeah, it looks like ninety percent of Ontario.* True enough.

As I'm staring at it a second message buzzes in. **Hi Perry. This is Gil. I told Lief I'd send him pictures of some birds and he said I could send them to your phone. I hope that's OK. If you don't want me to, just let me know.**

Good old Lief. I made him memorize my cell number after the time he threw up in class, and the school unsuccessfully called our empty house all afternoon, while Lief sat on a chair in the office, leaning over an empty garbage can when I would have been more than happy to leave French class to pick him up. To make it easy for him to remember, we used "Call me Maybe" and added our own chorus that went "Hey, I want Perry, and here's her number ..." followed by my phone number. It was silly, and it was fun, and it was meant as a memory device for Lief to use for himself.

Did he sing my number to you? I ask Gil.

Carly Rae Jepsen should totally watch out.

Puke and pop songs. No wonder you want to correspond with my little brother.

Your brother's great.

I was already inclined to like Gil, and I like him a lot more now.

I also remember the resin owl. I tap the picture and zoom it on my screen.

Is this bird alive?

It once was.

So, like, fifty percent closer to the real thing than the owl?

I'd argue it's more like ninety percent. This thing actually flew once. There's a pause, then a new message. **This grackle, I should say. It's a grackle … in case Lief asks.**

I bet you anything Lief will already know.

Will you bet a milkshake? The Perryside Diner has the best milkshakes in Laurentian county. Winner buys for loser.

It's much easier to say yes to a milkshake three-hundred-and-eighty-eight kilometres away, than it is to a smoothie just down the block. Easier, because I know it will never happen.

I send him a thumbs-up.

He texts back **So, it's OK if I use this number to send more bird pics?**

I send him a second thumbs-up.

I'm all for enjoying the benefits of Perryside without ever having to leave home.

***

I'm coming back to school with my backpack a lot lighter and the front pocket stuffed with lollipops. "Your brother is one of our best customers!" the children's librarian told me and opened a new pack of lollipops to reward him.

As I approach my locker—*our* lockers, because Sata and I have lockers side-by-side—I recognize the straightness of Sata's spine, the glossy tumble of her hair, and the throatiness of her laughter. I quicken my steps. She couldn't come to the library with me because of a Diverse Student Union meeting, but it must have gotten out early. Maybe we can get a hot chocolate in the cafeteria and catch up. "Hey, Sata …"

She turns, and I stop, because the person who's making her laugh is Adam Penske. The one who told me I was a drag after my mom died. Who finally succeeded in making me leave the house by dumping me via text; sending me straight to Sata's where we made cookie dough together and ate half of it raw and I said "Who needs guys anyway?" and she said, "Hang on, let's not be rash …" and we giggled until I decided I never liked Adam that much anyway.

"He has severe eyebrows," I'd told Sata and that had made her laugh so hard she'd snorted cranberry-pomegranate juice out her nose.

The way Adam is looking at Sata, his eyebrows seem to have completely lost their severity.

"Hey Perry," Sata says. Her voice is too high. Adam draws his eyebrows together.

Even though I don't care, and I don't need him, and it's a boring old story well past its best-before date, my heart's going just a little bit too fast, and the locker Adam's leaning on is mine, and I really don't see any way I can ask him to move without my voice wobbling, and then Mr. Tidwell walks by.

"Oh!" I say. "Whoops! I need to ask Mr. Tidwell something about our summative. Be right back!"

I follow the teacher's retreating back around the corner into the stairwell. He goes down, toward his classroom, and I go up, to the very top floor, where I do a U-turn and go back down and, sure enough, when I get back to my locker I have the whole space to myself so I can spin the lock and grab my books for my first class after lunch just as the bell chimes.

Chapter Seven

It's not quiet, but it is peaceful.

The wind is a constant—not a gale, by any means, but stronger than a breeze—it rustles the grasses when we're in open areas and quivers the turning leaves as we weave through the woods.

The thrush's song—constant, pretty, light and twittering—is punctuated every now and then by the hooting of an owl. Unmistakable—no wonder it's a birdsong we ask even the smallest of children to imitate—with a haunting, melancholy tone. The happy thrush says, 'It's still so beautiful; such a sunny evening, and nice and warm,' while the sombre owl reminds me, 'It's going to be dark soon, and the cold weather's coming.'

North is happy, and that's the most important thing.

The question rises in my mind every time he takes a misstep, or we hit uneven ground, or his head bobs—*should I be riding him?*

But there's no mistaking the pricking and swiveling of his ears, the flaring of his nostrils, and the overall swing of his body—even if there's an odd hitch to his gait—he's engaged, interested, alive.

If I didn't ride him—to spare his leg—what would I be sparing it for? His racetrack days are behind him. He'll never walk into a show ring again. He has a life to live out and it'll be an accomplishment if every day of it can be happy.

So we forge ahead through the trails around the farm, which should be familiar but feel magical, enchanted, and possess maybe just the tiniest edge of danger—the thrilling kind of danger—as the sun sinks and dark sifts down through the blue of today's bright sky.

The far fence of the property is mostly woods, with a big clearing in the middle. There are often deer here, and it's a great place to bring green horses, or day-dreaming equestrians. The hope is to desensitize the greenies, and to remind the inattentive riders that horseback is no place for star-gazing.

Just like he lords it over the youngsters he gets turned out with, North knows no deer can threaten him. The most he ever does is flare his nostrils and whiffle in their direction as though to acknowledge, *You live here. That's cool with me.* But spook, or bolt—not North. Not ever.

Which is why I'm completely unprepared as we step out of the woods—the shadows of the last trees still sliding over North's rump—and a noise like I've never heard before—a combination of grinding, and shaking, and banging, all laced through with a roaring growl—erupts from a spot slightly to the right and just behind us, and North *goes.*

I wonder if this is how he used to come out of the starting gate; in an explosion so quick and powerful it swipes the air from my lungs, slams my heart against my ribcage, and snaps my head back.

Whiplash, I think first. Then, *Holy shit!* Then, *Stop him!* Then ...

Maybe not.

My pulse is beating double-tempo, head light, extremities tingling.

This is fun.

Oh, wow. It's not every day you get to ride a horse bred to run at full race pace. So, yeah, he's old, but he's really fit. And he's lame, but I can't feel it right now, in his headlong charge for safety. He's so, so fast.

Instead of straightening, I lean forward. Instead of checking the reins, I scratch his withers and, when I do that, his ear flicks back so briefly I would have missed it if I'd blinked, and his neck takes on a tighter bow, and he surges—even faster; just for a couple of strides—until the guilt smacks me.

Wrong. This is so wrong.

What am I doing?

"Easy," I say.

Both ears swivel to me.

I smooth my hand down his neck. "You're fine."

We're running out of clearing, and North's running out of adrenaline.

His pace slackens.

"Good boy."

Hand gallop. Canter. Trot.

A horrible, jagged trot. *Short-short-short-short ...*

I suck in my breath. "Oh. I'm so sorry, boy."

He shakes his head and snorts and I laugh. "Yeah, you're right. It was worth it."

I hope. *I-hope, I-hope, I-hope, I-hope* becomes the rhythm of our ride back to the barn.

***

Smell so sharp it prickles the inside of my nose. The liniment's cold on my fingertips and North's legs are cool, too, as I rub it in. For *now* they are.

I cross my fingers quickly—*please let them be OK*—and don't uncross them until the thought's all the way through my mind.

There. That's the best I can do. Strong liniment and crossed fingers. The rest is up to North and Fate.

"Who's having a rubdown?" Clara comes around the corner sniffing the air like a hunting dog.

I look up. "We had a little run."

Clara's eyebrows arch. "An unexpected run? That's unlike him."

"There was a …" I shrug. "I don't know what. Some horrible noise like I've never heard before, like *he's* never heard before."

Clara's nodding. "From next-door."

"Yes! What was it?"

She shrugs. "Something the developers are doing. I don't know all the equipment they have."

"Developers? What do you mean, developers?"

She snaps her fingers. "I forgot—one of my Saturday students brought it out here the weekend you were away …" She fumbles on the corkboard, moving aside a flyer for a massage therapy course and an ad posted by somebody selling a pair of field boots. "I didn't know what to do with it, so I stuck it here." She tugs a brochure off the board and hands it to me.

Live the Mahogany Lifestyle it says, followed by paragraphs touting "a perfect blend of tranquility and convenience," promising "Beautifully landscaped parks and green spaces, steeped in natural features, and designed to be admired," and listing homes named, "Walnut," "Juneberry," "Aspen," "Elm," "Hazelnut," and "Ironwood."

There's a picture of rows and rows of tall, narrow houses clustered cheek-by-jowl with trees behind them. My jaw drops when I see the "affordable," prices.

"Is this for real?" I ask Clara.

She sighs. "Unfortunately, it is. That strip of land between us and the highway's been for sale for a while. I would have loved to buy it—not because it's particularly nice—but because I was afraid of this. These days anything with direct access to the highway is considered close and convenient. I knew it wouldn't be long before a developer snapped it up."

"But, tranquility ...?"

"I know," she says. "Only until they come out here with their big machines, right?"

North nudges me as though to say, *"Why are you still crouching down there, instead of standing up here giving me carrots?"*

I wobble, put a hand down, and laugh.

It's a forced laugh, though. This horse, and his well-being have been my responsibility ever since my mom got sick.

Knowing he was happy here was such a comfort. During the last few months of my mom's illness, with so much going on, I was relieved North wasn't one of the things I had to worry about.

He gives me another nudge that tells me the main thing he's worried about right this moment is still where his next carrot is coming from and, for now, I'm willing to go along with that.

Chapter Eight

I walk in the door to alarm bells.

Visual alarm bells, that is. A pot on the stove—the gas left on low—I flick it off. Dishes, not just dirty, but not even cleared off the table—very unlike Justin.

Water whooshing through the pipes over my head draws me toward the stairs. On the hall table a couple of envelopes, jagged tears in the end, letters scattered across the surface. At the foot of the banister a discarded t-shirt on the floor. The shirt I got Lief for his birthday; green, with a T-Rex roaring across the front. I know before I pick it up that it will be slimy with Lief puke. I pull it up by the corners; hold it out from my body as I mount the steps.

"Hey! I'm home! You guys up here?"

Justin's coming out of the bathroom with a towel-wrapped Lief in his arms. Lief's cheeks are flushed an angry red. He grinds his face against Justin's shoulder. "Daddy made the bath too hot, Perry." His voice is a long, low, whine. "Now I'm dizzy."

"I know you are buddy. You sometimes get dizzy when you throw up."

"No!" He shakes his head. "It was Daddy's fault. He didn't run the bath right."

"Lief," Justin says. "You know how to make this better. You have to go to sleep."

Justin's already walking toward Lief's bedroom and Lief talks over his shoulder to me. "Don't wanna go to sleep. I'll be dizzy in my bed."

"Do you want a cool facecloth on your forehead?"

He pushes his lip out. "Not from you. Not from either of you. I only want it from Mom."

Justin's shoulders stiffen and he hesitates for the smallest of seconds before continuing into Lief's room.

I turn back to the bathroom to run cold water over a facecloth. When I get back to Lief's room he's still flushed, still moaning, still whining, without saying much that makes any sense. Most importantly, he's flat on his back with Justin pulling the covers up around him.

I perch on the side of the mattress and smooth the cloth over the skin above Lief's eyebrows and he twitches. "Nuh-uh."

I hold it firm under my hand. Justin gives me a faint nod, then steps away from the bed and turns out the light.

"I. Said. No. Perry."

"I know you did."

"I don't want it, Perry."

"I know you don't."

"I only want Mommy to do it."

There's only one reason I'm able to stay confident and calm, and that's because I know I'm doing exactly what I need to for Lief. Exactly what my mom would have done. I know, because this is where she used to sit. The room would be dim, like this, and she'd press the cloth to Lief's forehead. I'd sit on the floor next to the bed and use the light spilling in from the hall to read out *The Cremation of Sam McGee*, and I'd keep reading long after my brother's mouth fell open, because there was something magical in the warmth and comfort of those moments.

I take a deep breath and force my voice to hold flat and even as I answer. "I know you do."

"I hate you, Perry."

"I know."

He blinks. His eyes fix on my face, then slide to the side. He blinks again. His eyes close and he whispers. "I love you, Perry."

"I know," I say.

I sit, in the dark room, and stare at the shaft of light from the hall slicing across my knees, and I count to fifty. I listen to the tick-tick-whoosh of the furnace cycling on. With my free hand I smooth Lief's quilt and something crinkles under my touch. When I move it into the light I recognize a print of the photo Gil sent. Lief's eyes flutter and he reaches out. "C'n I hold the grackle?"

When I hand it to him, he sighs, and turns his head sideways on the pillow, and within seconds he's breathing softly through slightly parted lips. I lift the facecloth from his forehead and stand up and walk out of the warm, quiet room.

Justin's in the hall. He takes the damp, no-longer-cool facecloth from my hand. "I'm sorry," he says. "You shouldn't have to do that. That's not the way it's supposed to be."

"And just when," I ask him, "was the last time things were the way they were supposed to be?"

***

Turns out the food left in the pot on the stove was my dinner. And turns out it's pretty good.

"Sorry," Justin says. "It was chili, but I'm afraid it's thickened up. Now it's more like a tomatoey-kidney bean paste."

"I like it." The truth is, I like sitting at the kitchen island, eating straight out of the pot. I like the warmth of the room, and the way the hot dishwater is steaming up the kitchen window. I like that Lief is deeply asleep and will feel better when he wakes up—he always does. I like that I got to see North, and I only have a little bit of home-work, and it's English ... and I like English.

For this suspended moment, everything is fine.

Justin collects the miscellaneous dirty dishes left on the island and ferries them to the counter next to the sink. "So. Speaking of things not being the way they're supposed to be ..."

Oh. The bubble of *fine* I've been sitting in dissolves.

My current mouthful of chili suddenly does feel quite gluey. I swallow it with effort, and say, "Yes?"

He turns to me and runs a hand through his hair. Maybe it's the dampness from his dish washing, or the light directly over his head, but suddenly his hair looks thinner. And has his hairline receded too? Just because I know Justin's got to be stressed, doesn't mean I want to face it. I drop my eyes to the remaining chili, most of which is burned to the bottom of the pot.

"Some letters came today."

Oh yeah. Papers scattered across the desk. A whiff of puke in the air. That seems like a long time ago now.

"Mm-hmm?"

"Do you want the good news first, or the bad news?"

I've never understood people who take good first—wouldn't they rather get the bad stuff out of the way and have something good to look forward to? "Bad," I say. "Lay it on me."

Justin leans back against the counter. "Lief's EDP centre is closing."

It's almost more of a shock than when my mom died. In one way, it *is* more of a shock, in that once I understood my mom's pancreatic cancer diagnosis, I knew she'd die before I'd expected her to—even if I didn't know exactly when. This, though—Lief was supposed to go to his centre until he started school. There was never a thought that he wouldn't. "It's impossible."

"No." Justin shakes his head. "Unfortunately, it's not. Their lease is up this year, and they haven't been able to negotiate a renewal at an affordable rent."

Affordable. Not only is Lief's daycare great, it's also subsidized. Justin makes a good salary, but even in a country with universal healthcare, cancer is expensive. Hospital beds, prescriptions for experimental drugs, and funerals are just a few of the things our family had to pay for that are way more expensive than you'd ever think they could be. The financial aspect makes the closing a double whammy. I swallow. "So, that's it? When? How ...?"

"End of the month. And 'how'—like do you mean how are we going to manage?" He shrugs. "I have no idea. I just ..." The hand goes through his thinning—greying, too—hair. He doesn't finish the sentence, but he doesn't need to. I, also, just don't know, or just can't imagine, or whatever "just" he was going to say. Like I said before, it's impossible. Unless …

"Wait. What was the good news?"

Maybe the good news is there's a new daycare centre opening up even closer to us. Maybe the good news is Justin's globe-trotting mother has been hit with maternal longings and is pausing her current round-the-world junket to stay with us for a while and help take care of her grandson. Maybe Justin won the lottery.

Even though he doesn't play the lottery.

Still …

Justin's voice startles me back to the real world. "You know the house in Perryside?"

As if I could forget the throwback house decorated in the colour palette of the fifties—or the seventies—or, more like a combination of the two. The single bathroom on the ground floor, the ancient appliances. The *storm* windows. For a second Gil flits into my mind, then right back out again, because his live, contemporary, good-looking vibrancy really does not fit, in any way, with the rest of my impressions of Perryside. "What about it?"

"It's yours."

Chapter Nine

Good news, Justin called it.

I get it. I see how he'd think it is—see how most people would think it is—to me, though, it's something else.

Not bad news, exactly, but *pressure*.

Pressure to feel a certain way, to react a certain way. Pressure to know what to do with this news which, in itself is complicated because, of course, it's nice to inherit something—especially when that something is a riverside property in a pretty town (even if the house that sits on it is decades out of date)—but I'm only inheriting it because my mom can't. Aunt Isabelle left it to her, and she's gone, so it comes to me.

And I don't know what to do about it.

I'm also pretty sure I know what Justin would do it if was his, and that makes it hard for me to meet his eyes.

He'd move there in a heartbeat, and I have the power to make that happen, and I won't be doing that.

And I love Justin.

So, good news? More like complicated news.

"Whoa," I say. "Wow," I say. I try to smile.

"It's a lot to take in," Justin says.

"It really is." I give an elaborate yawn. Stretch my arms. "Guess I'd better get to bed."

Justin nods. "Off you go. You have a lot going on."

He doesn't ask what I'm going to do about the house. He doesn't point out that it's an hour before my normal bedtime, and tomorrow's a PD day, so I can sleep in, so there's really no need to rush off to bed.

Justin, as always, considers my needs and my feelings.

It makes me want to do the same for him—but I'm just not sure if I can.

Chapter Ten

The last time I was at the barn I warned Karen, "I'll be here on Friday," and showed her the school board's online schedule. "See, it's a PD day—no school."

"Hmpf," she said. "Just so happens Friday was the day I was going to strip the stalls."

I'd laughed and flexed my arms, "Bring it on. Better than Chemistry any day."

Better than sitting around trying to figure out what to do about owning a house I'm not sure I want.

Thank goodness for the distraction offered by the barn, and North, and Karen and Clara.

The day is cold, but dry, and the sun's out, and all I have to do before heading to the barn is get Lief to his extended day program.

He looks fine following the drama of last night's bedtime. The only mark on him is a big pillow crease on his cheek.

When I put his porridge in front of him, I press my hand against his forehead. The skin is cool and smooth.

He swipes at my hand. "Don't do that!"

"I need to make sure you're OK."

"'Course I'm OK." When life gets to be a bit too much for Lief his body takes him out with a good puking session that leads to an early bedtime. He's always fine in the morning and, because he can't remember feeling sick, is completely intolerant of anyone who wants to pamper him.

"Fine," I say. "You do you. I'll do me."

I sit down at my own spot and peel an orange and listen to the radio. Traffic's bad. Of course it is. But that will be on the way into the city. I'm heading out.

The weather comes on. It might not get above zero all day.

"Whoa bud, it's going to be a cold one." I balance several orange slices on the edge of Lief's bowl. "Eat these up while I go dig out your warm clothes."

A sunbeam slants across my shoulders as I rifle through the bins in the side entrance. It warms me through. I find Lief's favourite dinosaur-patterned toque and one of the mitts that go with it.

I hum along to the familiar radio morning show music and paw around for the second dinosaur mitt.

"Ah-ha!" I pull it from the bottom corner of the bin.

"What is it, Perry?" Lief asks.

I step back and wave the dinosaur hat and mitts at Lief. "Look what I found!"

Lief rocks his chair back from the table and wiggles to the floor. He runs to me, takes the mitts, slides his hands into them, then lifts them both up. "Pull the mitts off!"

"Excuse me?"

"Pull them off, Perry!"

I shrug, pinch the tip of each mitt, and whisk them off my little brother's hands.

I gasp. In his right hand is something brilliant blue. I recognize it instantly as an origami bird. My mom taught herself to make them, and would tuck them away in secret places to satisfy Lief's bird-mania.

Lief chuckles. "I *knew* it would be there!"

I grab my brother in a fierce hug. Everything is here. My little brother, and pieces of my mother, everywhere. My heart is right here and I'm not letting go of it.

Lief roars in my ear. "Perry! You. Are. Crushing. Me!"

He stomps and wriggles and I release him. I guess sometimes practicality has to triumph over sentimentality.

It doesn't stop me from landing one last kiss on his forehead before he runs off, though.

* * *

There's a miraculous lack of traffic on the highway, and I fly along, and belt out the lyrics to my music, and trigger little bolts of happiness by thinking about that origami bird, and daydream about my horse so I won't think about dropping Lief off at daycare and wondering where he'll go after they close, and so I won't remember the stress on Justin's face, and so I won't circle back to the shifty, uncomfortable looks on Sata and Adam's faces when I ran into them at my locker.

I gear down, and make the turn onto the stable road, and even my favourite Arkells song on the stereo can't keep me smiling, because the surface is covered with chunks of thick mud shed by the tracks of a bulldozer and a gash has been opened through a tract of hardy jack pines with a sign staked by a rough-cut road promising **Wide lots! Custom designs! Executive living starting from the low five-hundreds!**

The last couple of times I've come out, the sun's already been pretty low in the sky. It all looks much worse in the stark morning light.

At least the barn driveway with its close-growing press of cedars is sheltered and unchanged. I trundle through the series of gates, closed every time we host a horse trial to ensure nobody can drive right through the middle of the cross-country course in use. I creep by Clara's signs posted at regular intervals beside the long drive that say, first **Speed Limit 18 3/4**—"Because everyone just rounds twenty up to twenty-five," Clara says—then, **For Fox Sake Reduce Your Speed** and, ending with a gentle,

Enjoy the Moment, Slow Down. That one always reminds me to ease my breathing, and my pulse, and puts me in the right frame of mind to see my horse.

I pull into my parking-spot-that-isn't-quite-a-parking-spot which I like because I can roll the car right under the spreading branches of a maple that, in the summer, keeps the interior from becoming an absolute oven while I ride, and at this time of year will let me come back to perfect red leaves dotted all over the roof and hood.

Just before I open the car door, my phone pings and I swipe the screen to find another message from Gil. **Today's feathered friend.** Even I recognize the black-capped adorableness of a chick-a-dee. It appears to have been photographed in the same spot, with the same leafy background, as the grackle, and it also appears to be slightly too stiff for life.

Should I be worried about where you're getting all these stuffed birds?

I believe the correct term is taxidermied.

That really doesn't make it sound any better.

It's a long story. Do you think it will bother Lief? Because, if so, I can stop sending them.

I think of Lief, clutching the photo of the stuffed taxidermied grackle. I realize I'm smiling a real, and true, unforced-by-loud-music smile for the first time this morning. **No. Please don't stop. The pleasure they bring outweighs the somewhat conflicted, mildly creepy feeling I have about taxidermy.**

Well, since you like it that much … how could I stop?

I will now be on pins and needles to see what other taxidermied specimens you have access to.

You just wait …

I'm still smiling as I walk across the gravel to the barn doors. Who knew a bunch of no-longer-living birds could be such a pick-me-up? I'm ready to think only good thoughts for several hours.

I step into the barn, which is only half-swept, and that's good because I can help Karen finish her work after I remind her there's no school today and I'm allowed to be here. If she wants to strip stalls I'm good with that.

"Yoo-hoo!" I call, and Karen immediately appears in a stall door, and she has a terrible expression on her face, and I count the stall doors between me and her again, just to make sure, but I already know it's North's stall.

Chapter Eleven

The good news is, Karen's not going to interrogate me about showing up in the middle of the school day.

The bad news is, it's because North is cast in his stall.

Shit.

He hasn't done this for so, so long.

He hasn't done this since he moved back here.

But he's done it now—no doubt about it. He's on his side with his legs tucked into a narrow space in the corner of his stall and, as I watch, panic sweeps him. He flails—as much as he can in the confined area. His hooves thud on the walls—fortunately without too much force, since he's now so thoroughly wedged—but I have no idea how long he's been down, or how hard he kicked on his way into this tight spot.

His neck is dark with sweat, and his eyes are too wide, and if he's been down for any length of time, we could have bigger problems.

To say I'm worried is an understatement, but at least I'm not panicking.

Unlike Karen.

The normally matter-of-fact, take-charge dynamo is rambling. "... had a dentist's appointment ... just got here ... found him like this ... Clara's out, checking fence lines ..."

"Karen," I say. "Karen!"

She stops talking and turns to me. "Call the vet," I say.

She blinks. I reach around, pull the receiver out of her back pocket, and put it in her hand. "Call the vet, tell her what's happened, and I'll be right back."

I walk to the end of the aisle, to where lengths of lead ropes hang from big hooks. I bypass all the thin, nylon ones and choose a couple of thick braided types.

I know how to do this. I know what to do. I know what not to do. I've seen it done before.

Back at the stall door I take a deep breath. Karen's on the phone with the vet. "... on his side ... cast ... sweating quite a bit ... twenty-five years old ..."

The instructions run through my head.

This is dangerous.

Always have a clear exit.

Don't trust him.

I know even somebody who's never afraid of horses should be scared of a cast horse. Because he's terrified, and each of his legs is a weapon, and as soon as they get free there are four of them that could strike me.

So I'm healthily fearful as I go in.

Try to help him help himself.

"Hey buddy, buddy. It's me, and I'm here. I'm going to help you, but I need you to stay calm ..." Meaningless repetition, just so he can hear my voice. Just so I can hear my voice.

I bend over by his neck—the least dangerous part of him—and I lace my fingers through big chunks of his mane—one about a third of the way down from his poll, the other about a third of the way up from his withers—then I lean back and tug. Grunt. Haul. Heave.

"Come on, baby!" His body moves. A bit. Not enough. As quickly becomes clear when hope surges through him and he scrambles as much as he can, and his hooves hit the wall with a force that could easily break a human rib, and he still can't get up, and his hope turns to desperation. I want so badly to lay my hand on his neck—to help him calm down, but if he somehow gets free right now, I'll be right in the path of his hooves.

So I have to wait.

And talk. "As soon as you calm down, I'll help you again. It'll be fine. We'll get you up, but you just have to chill for a minute, so I can come closer to you."

When he's still again, except for the heaving of his side, and an occasional twitch of his ear, I step forward.

"Perry ..." Karen's off the phone. "Maybe you should wait for the vet."

I shrug. "Somebody's got to go in there to help him. He's my horse, so it should be me. The vet's for after."

And may we not need her. I'll happily pay a call-out fee for her to just give North a once-over and pronounce him completely fine.

If I can get him up.

"Roll the door open as wide as it will go," I tell Karen.

With my escape route as big, and clear as possible, I walk back over to North. Talking, talking, talking. Touching his back, running my hand along his body, until I'm at his hind end.

His ear is on me. "Just lie still," I order … plead … pray.

I try as hard as I can not to hold my breath while I do the scariest thing of all. Leaning forward, passing the rope under his leg, bringing it up on the other side and crossing the two ends in my closed fist so there's a loop of rope for me to pull on.

Now to do the same thing on his foreleg. I'm not as scared up by his head where I can see his eye—where he can see me. His bottom foreleg isn't pressed tight against the boards and I'm able to dangle the loop and catch the foreleg through it.

And now …

I take a deep breath, move to a point behind the middle of his body, check my footing, lean back and pull for all I'm worth. Pull with everything I've got. Just when I'm not sure I have anything more to pull with I feel a pull around my own waist. Karen, bless her. It's not that she helps physically, but knowing she's there I give one more strong effort, and North does the same, and he's up, onto his back, almost coming over.

Almost ... almost ... almost ... If I let go too soon, he'll just fall back, but if I wait too long those flailing legs will come over toward me.

"Back up!" I warn Karen, and she goes. I count, *three-two-one ...* then I go, too, twisting and scooting out the door with Karen sliding it closed behind me, and turning back just in time to see my big, grey boy lurch to his feet.

I feel like he must feel. Elated and depleted. Like I could climb a mountain, and like my legs are going to shake right out from under me.

Karen's clapping my back. "Where did you learn to do that?"

"I watched my mom do it."

"Lucky thing," she says.

I shake my head and blink hard. "Yeah. Lucky."

Except I remember what my mom said to me afterward. "This won't do, Perry. The next time he could really hurt himself. We can't leave him here."

***

North's fine.

"He'll probably have some sore spots," the vet says. "Imagine how you'd feel if you got yourself into a similar position, and exerted that much effort, and you were over seventy years old. Obviously if there's a particularly sore area, or swelling, you can call me, but I wouldn't overly worry if he's slightly ouchy all over for a couple of days."

It's the best I could have hoped for.

No, it's even better because the vet waved off my offer to pay. "I was coming by later today anyway, to check over those two new geldings Clara brought in, so I just moved my appointments around. No big deal."

She turns expectantly to Clara, who arrived in from her fence check after all the excitement was over.

"Sure. I'll show them to you now." Clara pauses, and turns to me. "Are you around all day?"

I nod. I expect her to assign a string of misbehaving school horses and greenies to me. Instead she says, "Maybe we can go for a hack later?"

It sounds nice. Hacks are nice. But Clara's far too busy to go for a casual hack with me just for the heck of it. There's more to this. I don't want to find out—don't want to go. I nod again. "Sure. That would be good."

I spend the rest of the morning emptying the stalls all around North of bedding, which allows me to glance into his stall every five minutes and make sure he's breathing, hasn't spontaneously started bleeding, and is still standing on all four feet. The first few times I look in, he sweeps his ears forward and gives me the deep nicker which, as a human, I interpret as affection, but which I'm pretty sure in horse actually means, "Hey, have any carrots for me?"

By the fourth or fifth check-in he's tired of me and barely interrupts his doze to flick an ear in my direction.

When Clara strolls by and says, "Why don't you saddle up Titan?" I rouse North first and turn him out because at least in his paddock he can't get cast.

Half an hour later Clara and I are heading down the driveway—she's on a pretty little bay mare who's holding her head unnaturally high and swiveling her ears at everything. My awkwardly gawky gelding plods along with all the grace of a Star Wars AT-AT and about the same level of animation. "These two both came from that stable downtown," Clara tells me. "No turn-out and no hacking. When we were schooling cross-country last weekend, this one—" She points down at her mount, "—wouldn't go through a gate. Gotta get them used to everything in the country before the next eventing season starts."

Which, yes, is true. But also is definitely not the reason we're out here with me freezing my hands off because a) I couldn't find my winter riding gloves and b) it's not winter, so I shouldn't need gloves yet. Unfortunately, you can't logic yourself out of so-cold-they-won't-move fingers, so it's actually a good thing that my rock-steady mount requires very little contact.

Clara and I seek out every single thing that might make a horse accustomed to downtown living look twice. We go to the clearing where the deer always hang out, and surprise two. They stare at us, fine heads alert, wide ears backlit pink by the sunlight glowing through them. We splash through the stream that criss-crosses the property. We ride to the end of the driveway and wait until one of the massive construction vehicles lumbers by, rattling gravel and dropping mud clods.

After her mare's done a nervous turn-on-the-forehand, and calmed herself by pushing her face against my gelding's neck, Clara sighs, and I think, *Here we go*. The true reason for this ride is about to be revealed.

She detaches her mare from my gelding, and says, "Come on. I want to try her through that gate again." When I catch up and the two horses are walking side-by-side again, she says, "It's about North."

Of course it is.

"Thank goodness he's OK."

I nod. "Yes. Thank goodness."

"There have been other things, though."

I think of his uncharacteristic bolt the other day. "Like what?"

"He's been ... maybe not full-on stall-walking, but sometimes he's restless in his stall. And did you notice the bare spot on his chest? He's been rubbing against his stall guard so we've had to shut his door, which probably, in turn contributes to the walking ..."

I twist a hunk of the gelding's mane around my fingers. These things aren't new. Clara knows they aren't new. They're a big part of the reason we moved North here—these are the things he used to do at his previous barns.

I look at her. "So, what do you think?"

"I would say to turn him out more, but ..." She waves toward the highway—toward the construction zone between us and the highway. Even though we're on a trail through the forest, buffered all around by close-growing evergreens, there's a constant low background grind of machinery.

"Yeah. *But* ..."

"The thing is, Perry, it's going to be months and years of this. And they're not even building on the section closest to our property yet."

Months and years of disruption for my twenty-five-year-old horse. A lot of horses his age don't have months or years left to live, period. I'm thinking of North living out the rest of his life next to a massive construction site.

"Do you have a suggestion?" I ask.

She sighs again. "I wish I did."

The trail narrows, and her mare naturally surges forward, with my mellow gelding following behind. Clara half-turns. "Maybe he just needs some time. Maybe it's an adjustment he'll make."

"Maybe," I say. *No way on earth*, I think.

"There's also ..."

I don't know if her voice has trailed off because she's in front of me and has to pay attention to something on the trail, or if she's reluctant to continue. The path widens and I urge my lackadaisical gelding forward. "Also, what?"

"Well, there's Ace. The vet mentioned it. It's not that she's recommending it—and I'm not either—but it's a possibility we should at least pass on to you. It could take the edge off. It might help."

The words tumble out of her in a very un-Clara-like manner. She was nervous to bring it up. For good reason. My horse lifts his head and spurts forward and it's entirely a reaction to the tension flooding my body.

I stroke his neck. "I'm sorry." I take a deep breath so I don't cause the same reaction in Clara who, after all, is just trying to help. But I am *not* sedating my horse.

"I can see why you and the vet would mention it ..."

"But you don't want to do it."

I shake my head. "If you take North's edge way, you take away what makes him North."

"I know."

I know, too. I know what she's thinking, but not saying. That if you take away one of North's legs because he gets cast again and breaks it against his stall wall, he won't be North for long then either.

I know. Clara knows. We know each other knows, so there's no point in going over and over all the points.

I open my mouth to say I'll think about it, but before I can get the first word out, she's gone.

Her mare has exploded in a sideways-leaping bolt and if Clara had a less rock-solid seat, or shallower heels, she'd be on the ground right now.

I know the best thing the gelding and I can do is stop and stand and be solid and safe, so that's what I do. No horse could be more unconcerned than the one I'm on, and that definitely helps Clara as she finally pulls the terrified mare to a halt.

Trying to ride her back is another matter. She dithers—rocking back and forth from one foot to the other.

I walk the gelding over and bring him up beside her. She presses in close to his calming bulk and steps forward with him but, even then, there's a point beyond which she just won't go. *No way, never,* say her stiff forelegs and her head held so high it's nearly in Clara's face.

"Great, she's actually getting worse. We didn't make it anywhere near the gate this time."

"Hmm …" I look at the gate, about fifty feet to our right. I look at the direction of the mare's ears and her flaring nostrils. "Were you riding at it this way on the weekend, or from the other side?"

"The other side. Why?"

"I just …" I nudge the gelding forward.

"She's not going to come," Clara says.

"No, I know. Not yet, anyway." I ride right up to a tree next to the trail, then with a combination of leg and hip, convince the gelding to leg yield until he's underneath the spreading branches. I knot the reins, rest them on his withers, warn him to "Whoa," and bring my knees up to my armpits and my feet to the saddle.

"Perry!" Clara calls.

"Don't worry, he's rock solid, and anyway … I just …" I half-stand until I can grab the branch I want, then pull myself into the right position. "Whoa," I remind my dozy mount and, holding what I want, lower myself back into the saddle and ride out from under the branches.

The mare immediately steps forward toward the security of her friend and Clara says, "What the heck is going on?"

"Hold on," I warn her.

"What?"

I pull the thing I plucked from the tree out of my jacket and the mare stops dead and gives a rattling snort. I quickly tuck it back out of sight. "It wasn't the gate she was afraid of."

Clara furrows her brow. "Is that a plastic owl?"

I laugh, "Actually, I think you'll find it's resin. But, yes."

* * *

Back in the barn, as we untack the horses, Clara's regaling Karen with our resin-owl adventures. "You should have seen Perry. She was standing on Titan's back."

Karen sticks her head out of a stall and gives me a look. "Just think of it as voltige," I suggest.

"Anyway, Karen, we're going to have to buy a dozen of those owls. We'll slather one in molasses and put it in the middle of her grain. We'll put them all over the barn. We'll desensitize the heck out of her."

I listen to the excitement in Clara's voice and I think this is why North has been so happy here. Because Clara loves finding ways to meet her horses' needs and keep them happy.

The good news is, she probably can get the mare to the point where she'll accept having an owl in her stall, and will probably even walk right by the one in the indoor arena.

The bad news is, the mare will probably always dislike owls. Horses' instincts are deep, often mysterious, and hard-wired. Even if she eventually walks up to owls strategically placed around Clara's barn, and nuzzles them, I still wouldn't trust her at a strange property, on a new course, seeing one in an unexpected moment.

And that's the exact same reason I can't pretend this huge development next to Clara's isn't going to be a massive problem for North. We can do everything and anything we want. We can try to comfort him in every way we can think of. But as long as the big machines are roaring around on what he thinks of as his property, my horse isn't going to be happy.

Which is a very big problem.

***

I'm on the final approach to my house, driving through the neighbourhood I've taken for granted my whole life.

Where, if it wasn't for North, our family wouldn't really have needed a car. Where Lief and I can walk to school and daycare. Where Justin is just a short stroll to the subway to get to his family medicine practice, or to the hospital. Where we can run out of any ingredient for any meal at any time of day and just head out for a brisk walk and whatever it is we need.

At breakfast Lief ate the last of the yogurt. Justin would say don't worry about it. There are plenty of other things Lief can have for breakfast until we go grocery shopping again. But if my mom was still alive, she would definitely pop out and pick up an extra pint of yogurt. I like to make my little brother happy.

Plus, I like yogurt.

There just happens to be a big, easy-to-manoeuvre-into parking spot right down the street from the corner store—which would be a little like me going to catch North and finding a unicorn in his paddock—so I take it as a sign, and slide the car alongside the curb and go to get a pint of yogurt for Lief and me.

Because of where they're sitting, I don't see them on the way there. On the way back to the car I'm humming to myself because I got black cherry yogurt, which I really, really like, and because at least North wasn't hurt after being cast, and Clara was so happy about me figuring out the mare's problem. My heart's lifting, and I'm hoping we'll find a way to keep North happy at the barn, and that's when I see them.

Sata and Adam. Who would normally add to my happiness. Who would wave me into the smoothie bar and insist that I try the Smoothie of the Day, and make me laugh by doing impressions of the very nasally voice and mournful expression of the school librarian.

Except they don't wave me in, because they don't see me, because it's hard to see other people when you're both leaning so far across the table that you're practically rubbing noses, and your eyes are locked on each other and, oh yeah, just to make sure there's no way I can explain it away, there are their hands, fingers intertwined, on the table beside their smoothies.

My stomach clenches. I'm suddenly really cold.

I need to get home. I need to put my yogurt in the fridge. I need a shower. A really hot one. I need my little brother to be happy, and my horse to be OK, and my world to be right.

I need my mom.

Chapter Twelve

When I get out of the shower, the world's gone dark earlier than normal with low-hung rain clouds obscuring the last bit of the daylight. I put on pyjama pants, snug my still-wet hair in a scrunchie and my comfort-seeking mind turns to homemade mac n' cheese.

That'll do it. That'll fix everything—at least for tonight.

It doesn't even matter that there's no old cheddar in the fridge because on nights like this I go to the chest freezer downstairs. We've worked our way through most of the casseroles that neighbours and friends dropped off in the wake of my mother's death—lasagnas, and chicken and rice casseroles, and shepherd's pie—but there's also a precious stash of my mom's classic mac n' cheese, that she made herself, and that I've defrosted very sparingly.

I'll grab one, defrost it, and put it in the oven while I start work on my geography summative—trying to explain how home is where my horse is without thinking too hard about my horse's apparent unhappiness with his current home.

The basement is unfinished. It was always a thing Justin and my mom talked about doing after Lief was born. So we'd have an extra space in the house to spread out. They pictured Lief with a bunch of hyper primary school buddies bouncing around a downstairs playroom, while they enjoyed a civilized evening in the main floor living room. They pictured me upstairs having a teenage get-together in the finished attic space. I'm pretty sure they didn't picture my friends being more interested in each other than in me.

I throw open the lid of the chest freezer and look in the corner where we stacked all those casseroles. I find *Lasagna*, *Lasagne*, and *Lasagnae*. I don't want lasagna, though. I want mac n' cheese—and not just any mac n' cheese; I want my mom's mac n' cheese. I sort, and lift, and restack, and ... there isn't one.

I stare at the pile of foil-covered dishes. I look through them one more time. How could this happen? How could we have eaten the last of my mom's cooking, without me even *knowing* it was the last?

I know I need to close the freezer. I can hear my mom's voice reminding me, "If you leave the lid open the frost will build up." But I can't. I feel like closing the lid would be admitting defeat. I walk a tight circle and tighten my fists. I *want* there to be another mac n' cheese. It's not fair that there isn't.

I can see why Lief has temper tantrums. It feels good to be angry, and to shake a fist, and stomp my feet.

It feels better than crying, which is the clear alternative.

The floor above my head creaks. Justin and Lief coming home. Which means I should already have dinner in the oven.

I mutter one final curse into the air, grab a lasagna, and close the freezer.

***

Lief's come home wearing a pair of yellow rubber boots with black soles. I've never seen them before. "These are *not* my boots, Perry."

"I know, Lief."

"Somebody else took my boots, Perry."

"Is that what happened?"

He nods toward Justin who's standing in his coat with his phone pressed to his ear. "Daddy said so. He said somebody who didn't know any better wore my boots home and left these ones, so I had to wear these ones home and I don't even like them."

"I'm sorry that happened, Lief, and I'm really glad you were helpful and agreed to wear these boots home."

"Daddy said I had to. He said he couldn't carry me the whole way." Lief gives a dramatic sigh and blinks hard, and at the end of his day, when he's tired and hungry is the most precarious time of all, and it's much easier to stave off a temper tantrum than to get him to climb down from one.

"But Liefy ...?"

"Yeah?"

"Didn't you tell me your boots pinched your toes?"

"Um, yeah. But these ones do, too."

"OK, but you're not keeping these. We already know that. And what we could do is go to the store and get you some new boots that are bigger and they won't pinch your toes at all."

He blinks and rolls his shoulders back. "Could we get any kind of boots I want?"

"Any ones that fit you."

"Even ones like Hannah has, with unicorns on them?"

"If they have unicorn ones that fit you, you can have them. Or you can pick another pair that fit you."

Meanwhile, Justin's signing off. "I appreciate the offer. I'll have to run some numbers. When do I need to get back to you?"

Lief's pants are puddle-splashed so I wriggle them off and leave him standing in his underwear. "Run upstairs and put your pyjama pants on, and in a little while we'll have lasagna for dinner."

Justin slides his phone onto the counter, rubs his hand across his face, and turns a tired smile to me. "Thanks for helping with him."

"Not a problem." I hesitate, then point to his phone. "Hard day?"

He points to the oven. "It'll be OK now."

Of course he doesn't know the massive disappointment the lasagna in the oven represents to me. I bite my tongue and nod. "You're right."

***

Justin and I work side-by-side in friendly silence at the kitchen table while the lasagna bubbles in the oven and, in the next room, Lief watches his current favourite Mighty Machines DVD: At the Demolition Site.

The closing music blares out, and Justin asks, "How close are we?"

I look up. "Um, I was just going to toss the salad and set the table."

"Cool. I'll go get him to wash his hands."

The salad's ready and there are five minutes on the oven timer. I move my laptop off the table, then reach for Justin's. When I touch it the black screen glares to life.

Justin was working on a spreadsheet. The left-hand column lists: Property Taxes, Mortgage, Utilities, Phone, North Board, Daycare.

All the numbers are more than I expected. I really had no idea how high property taxes are. And the mortgage—well that got bigger when Justin and my mom decided it was smarter to add to the mortgage than to run up credit card debt to cover the extra expenses we had while she was sick. North's board … I do my best to reduce it by working at the barn whenever I can, but board costs for barns within forty-five minutes of downtown are expensive. And the daycare. That's the kicker. I know what Lief's daycare cost has always been, and the amount Justin has in the column is more than double what I expected.

That must have been the phone call he was on when he came home. Lief's been offered a spot at a new daycare and Justin's running the numbers.

They're not good. The number at the bottom is red. It's not small, either.

"Perry!" Lief, rosy-cheeked and pyjamaed, tackles my knees. "Are we having garlic bread?"

I laugh and turn to Justin. "If Justin can move his laptop so I can put these placemats down then, yes, I'll be able to put garlic bread on the table."

Justin says all the right things. How delicious the lasagna is. What a good caesar salad I made.

"It was a kit," I say.

"Was the garlic bread a kit too?" Lief asks. "Because it's really yummy!"

There's no mistaking how genuinely happy Lief is. There's no mistaking how hard Justin's trying to act happy.

After dinner Justin lifts a tomato-sauce smeared Lief down from the table. "Let's get you into the bath."

I say, "Mrs. Sharma made us that lasagna ages ago. I'm going to wash her dish now and walk it back to her."

Justin nods. "Tell her thank-you."

With Mrs. Sharma's still-warm Pyrex dish in a tote bag, I step into the starry cool of an autumn evening. The smell of leaves is in the air. Even though we're deep in the heart of a bustling city I believe I can smell campfire. On nights like this it's easy to imagine.

Of course, if I was in Perryside, I'd probably be smelling actual campfire.

Thinking of Perryside makes me think of the last time the three of us were all happy at the same time. Crazy it is that it was at a funeral, but there you go.

Funeral or not, my mind's full of the fresh air, and the towering trees. The quiet, endless space to run in. The horses just down the road. I remember Lief and Justin laughing a lot, and how every single thing made Lief's eyes open wide, and how there were no pushed-out bottom lips, or temper tantrums.

I remember how very, very well I slept.

I remember the glisten of tears in Justin's eyes as we drove out of town.

I hand Mrs. Sharma her dish back and deliver high praise for her cooking, then I head back home.

And that spurs a different train of thought. The thought that normally I'd just keep walking, right over to Sata's house. But now ... well ... I've worked pretty hard at pushing her away. Adam first, then her. And, I guess it worked. Adam is someone I really liked at one point, and Sata's someone I love, so it's no surprise they'd like each other. But given that they do, I don't really want to see them.

And they probably don't want to see me.

My next thought is of Justin, and how he seems to have aged years since we got back. Then of how hard it was for Lief to handle unfamiliar boots—how is he ever going to adjust to an unfamiliar daycare?

The problem with North is almost worse. If we could keep Lief at his current, perfect daycare we would. But the home that up until now was perfect for North, no longer is.

Then there's the money.

The thought that's tormenting me isn't "I wish I could fix it." The thought that's tormenting me is "I know how to fix it."

I can fix all of the above in one fell swoop. Take away the mortgage and the exorbitant property taxes. Remove the need for Lief to even go to daycare. Give North a new, and quieter home. Even leave Sata and Adam to grow their relationship in peace.

The only sacrifice is me. My home. The home where my mother surrounds me. I'd have to leave it behind.

I'm so torn I walk around the block an extra time so I can think a little more.

It doesn't help. When I come back in through the side door, bringing a gust of night air with me, I still don't know what to do.

Then I look across, to where Justin's got his laptop open on the kitchen table again, and I see the dark circles under his eyes, and I clear my throat.

When I open my mouth I'm not focused on details like where will Justin work, or what are the schools like. I'm turning a blind eye to Aunt Isabelle's terrible, terrifying dishwasher, which is only one example of the ancient state of the appliances in my aunt's house.

When I open my mouth I'm responding to how bone-tired Justin looks, and how much that scares me, and I say, "What if we moved to Perryside?"

He looks at me for several long seconds, then drops his face to his hands, rubs his fingers up, then down his forehead and meets my gaze again. "I was afraid you'd never ask."

Chapter Thirteen

Turns out, you can get rid of a lot of stuff in a few short weeks.

Turns out, you can leave an old life behind more quickly than I ever would have thought.

That's the thing about living in a central neighbourhood in a big city. People want to buy houses like ours. Even houses with unfinished basements that have a corner that gets wet when it rains hard, and floors that slant toward the walls, and windows that pour in cold air all through the winter.

It's because they're going to tear the house down and build something new with a glass staircase and flooring harvested from Oceanic mango.

I push that voice down, along with the one that asks me, if this house is being torn down, and if this is the last place I remember my mother ... what does that mean?

I silence those voices because I can't remember ever seeing Justin so happy. He heads off to work each morning, grinning from ear-to-ear at the prospect of interviewing bright young doctors keen to fill his place in his downtown family practice. Perryside, like many small and rural communities in the province, is perpetually short of family doctors, so the mayor of Perryside is tripping over himself to help set up Justin's new office there.

Lief is a chattier, bouncier, less tantrummy version of himself as well. Hannah's mother has taken a month of vacation to stay home with Hannah while they find her a new daycare, and Justin's paying her to watch Lief, too. Lief's current life is one big playdate and every night he talks to me about Perryside. "Daddy says he'll hang my curtains from this room in my new room there," "Daddy says we'll get a new bathtub in the Perryside bathroom so I can have a deep bath," and "I'm n'a ask Gil to show me a real owl."

Gil. Tall frame, broad shoulders, nice hair, kind voice.

A message came in this morning containing a picture of a bright red cardinal perched in front of the usual bushy background. It made me simultaneously happy and sad. There's nothing more gorgeous than a cardinal … but the one in the photo is dead.

Also, it's great to hear from Gil … but the message was actually for Lief.

Nothing in life comes without trade-offs.

Most people would say Perryside's trade-offs make this move worthwhile. It's beautiful. It's peaceful. North will be at Riverhaven farm, a short walk down the road. Justin's sister has a cottage there, and she also has kids around Lief's age, so we have cousins there—at least part-time.

I Googled the high school and they have some interesting courses. They have a co-op program. They have a working traffic light at a fake intersection behind the auto shop, erected so student drivers could practice for their driving tests in the days before Perryside got their current actual set of traffic lights on Upper Water Street.

I bet Justin practiced his traffic stops and starts there. I bet my mom did, too.

Of course, I'm leaving a place where I *know* all the things she did for sure—where I can remember her doing them. Backing the car out of the driveway to take me to the barn. Kneeling in front of the TV folding our laundry. Giving Lief his first baths in our big kitchen sink. Why am I trading sure memories for a whole bunch of uncertainty?

When questions like that pop into my head, I get busy packing.

We are very, very well packed.

***

The day comes. Which, of course, it always does.

Unless cancer gets you first.

In which case, the day still comes, it's just that you don't have to be the one who realizes that it was overly efficient—and quite inconvenient—to pack *all* the toilet paper, and that it would have been better to have told Justin which bag the trip snacks were in, so he didn't put it right at the back and bottom of the cargo space in our new-to-us SUV, and you also don't have to figure out how to say good-bye to the bedroom where you've cried yourself to sleep, and the kitchen where you've burned every single spatula in the drawer, and the living room ...

Justin finds me in the living room.

"Hey, Perry!" His footsteps and his voice are loud in the emptiness left behind now that we've sold, given away, shipped, or packed everything that used to be in the house. "Perry? You OK?"

I'm looking at the mantelpiece. It's nothing special. It's not even finished. And that's the point. My mom was going to re-finish it. She had plans for it. She'd asked me if I wanted to help—told me we'd listen to music and sand the terrible old paint off the wood—said I could pick the playlist.

I'd said something like, "Uh-huh-maybe-we'll-see-if-I'm-not-at-the-barn."

This mantelpiece doesn't hold a memory for me. But it could have.

Justin looks at me, looking at it. He was there for my lukewarm response to my mom's offer of a mother-daughter bonding activity.

He follows my eyes to the three splotches of colour painted off to the side. My mom's three suggestions. We were supposed to vote on them. I think Lief is the only one who did. I'm pretty sure he voted for each one, twice.

Justin reaches into his back pocket and fishes out a screwdriver—because if there's one thing I've learned, it's that on a day you're moving you really should carry a screwdriver around—then he steps forward and starts twisting a screw out of the mantelpiece.

"Wait … it screws in?"

"Yuh-huh." He hands me the first screw, which I never noticed before but now, of course, there's a big dark hole where it used to be. He moves onto the next one.

"And you're unscrewing it?"

"Yup." He hands me the second screw.

"But, the new people … won't they …?" I immediately regret asking because I don't want him to tell me they're probably taking possession with a bulldozer and an excavator.

He's not stupid, though. "It's not written into the agreement of purchase and sale, so it doesn't go with the house."

"Oh. OK." I accept the third screw from him. "What are we going to do with it?"

"For now—put it in the spare stall in the horse trailer. Bring it with us. Later—refinish it." The last screw comes loose and he gives the mantle an almighty bang, and when the whole thing tilts away from the wall he slings it over his shoulder. "Come on—you can let the ramp down for me."

And that's how, an hour later, we're taking over-cautious turns in the SUV we traded our hatchback in for, towing the secondhand horse trailer we bought from a family two streets over whose daughter left for university and sold her horse two months ago.

In the back of the SUV is my little brother, singing under his breath and reading road signs out loud, and in one stall of the trailer is my noble old horse, with our ancient mantelpiece secured with a lead rope in the stall next to him.

Justin merges us onto the highway, points at the sign confirming we're heading north, then he looks at me. I hold my breath, because I'm afraid he's going to ask, "Happy?"

If he did, I'd have no idea what to say.

Yes, and no, is probably the only thing that comes close.

Yes, for North, because living in Perryside is definitely going to be as peaceful as he could want it to be. No, though, because of the weight, and the hair he's been losing over these past few weeks as the bulldozers keep rumbling and his world keeps being turned upside-down.

Yes for Lief, because he's excited, and Justin's going to have flexible hours, so there won't be any need for day-care, but no because if we hadn't lost our mother we wouldn't be here.

Yes for Justin, because I know he needs the change, but no because of the circumstances that brought it about.

Yes for me because I didn't have much left in the city. After Sata came by and sat beside me on the porch and said, "About Adam ..." and I said, "Really, it's no big deal," and I realized I totally meant it—it was no big deal. I'd let go of both of them. I'll always wish her well, but Sata and I have drifted apart, the way Adam and I had already drifted apart. Which left me in a place where everyone I loved was unhappy.

Now everyone I love is speeding along the highway with me, and Justin isn't asking, "Happy?" he's saying, "Here we go."

I turn around and look all the way back to the trailer, then to my little brother, who's humming Skinnamarink, then turn to face Justin. I nod. "Here we go."

Chapter Fourteen

We arrive on Friday, as it's getting dark, and by Saturday it's like we've always lived here.

Or, correction, it's like the rest of them have always lived here.

North quickly shoves his way into a position of leadership amongst the herd of horses down the road.

Margaret—the woman who breeds the horses I've since learned are Canadians, and much sought-after by heritage sites, national parks, and general Canadian enthusiasts—has a well-banked stall and a full haynet ready for North's arrival. "He can go out in the morning," she says.

The morning finds me wishing I'd put on another layer, watching my breath mist in the cold air, shifting from foot to foot, stomach full of butterflies.

Margaret's herd is a uniform group of unblanketed, unclipped, untrimmed dark-coated horses with sturdy legs, natural manes and, from their universal head-down, grass-eating stance, not a care in the world.

North, by contrast, is all whiteness and brightness. I never felt like I could keep him clean enough back at Clara's, but here his exposed neck and legs seem to glow. When I bought it, I thought the bright teal stripe on the bottom of his turn-out blanket was cheerful, now it just looks kind of silly. His neatly pulled mane and closely trimmed fetlocks have a prim look to them.

And the way he's pushing his chest up against his stall door, ears pricked forward and nostrils flaring makes him look like the kid in kindergarten who really wants to make new friends but you just know half the kids in the schoolyard are going to beat him up, and the other half will ignore him.

I don't want my kid beaten up or ignored.

"Ready?" Margaret asks.

Margaret is to me what her horses are to North.

I've never thought of myself as delicate, or fragile, or a girly girl. If anything, because I ride horses, the kids in my city neighbourhood thought I was tough. Next to Margaret, though, in her oilskin coat, snowmobile pants, and steel-toed workboots, sporting a toque liberally adorned with shavings and hay, and wearing unmatched gloves, my tall gore-tex leather riding boots and padded vest quilted in a pattern of horses' heads seem fairly ridiculous.

I am ridiculous. My horse is ridiculous.

Except nobody's told him that.

"I ... um ... I'm not sure."

"What are you not sure about?" Margaret's tone isn't unkind. It's just matter-of-fact.

"Maybe I should turn him out in the round pen for today."

She shakes her head. "The round pen is for training. Not for turn-out."

"Maybe we should introduce him to the herd gradually."

"How would we do that?"

"Maybe I could graze him on this side of the fence for a while."

"Does he look like he wants to graze on this side of the fence?"

"I'm just concerned ... if they don't take to him ... he might bite. Or kick. I'd hate for him to hurt any of your horses."

"I'm not worried about my horses, my dear. They'll be fine." She holds up her hand. "And just in case what you're actually worried about is your horse getting hurt, no need. I breed for temperament. That's the most chill herd of horses you'll ever meet."

"Maybe I should go get his mid-weight blanket from the trailer. It's colder than I expected."

"Pfff ...!" Margaret reaches out and runs her hand down North's neck. "Do him good to let that coat thicken up. I'm not on board with all this over-blanketing horse owners have started doing—although I'm sure the blanket companies love it—the best insulation is natural insulation."

I want to throw in another "maybe," but I know Margaret will have an answer, and I know her answers are probably right.

I roll my shoulders back, lift North's halter off the hook on the outside of his door, and say, "Alright big boy. You can go meet your new friends."

He prances beside me all the way to the field gate, which is pretty much the way I imagine he used to prance his way along the track on the way to the starting gate more than twenty years ago.

The only thing that keeps him from shoving his way through the gate is the years and years of work first my mother, then I have done with him. You stand for the farrier. You stand while we mount. You stand until we take the lead off your halter.

I take the lead off his halter and he flares his nostrils, lets out a ringing whinny and trots into the field, knees and tail lifted in vivid reminder of the Arabian heritage running through all Thoroughbreds. When he turns up the flare like this it's harder to tell he's lame.

He circles the grazing Canadians, and as he goes by individual horses raise their heads to watch him. Their ears show a gentle curiosity. One or two return to grazing but most watch as he starts his second lap as though to say, "OK, you have our attention, what next?"

The *what next* is North breaking into a canter. He sweeps fairly close to one gelding who might even be the one I met the last time we were here. If he was a person, he'd shrug. Instead he does the horse equivalent—an easy side-to-side head shake—then he follows North in a swinging walk that pops up to a trot, and soon he's cantering behind him.

Others join in, one-by-one, until Margaret and I are standing by the fence watching a broad whirlpool of cantering bodies—all dark except for the punctuation of North's white head and legs. They use most of the open space in the field, and we can feel the thunder of their hooves through the ground when they pass us. Then, apparently satisfied at having driven everyone to join in his game, North slows to a trot, then walk, and drops his head to the grass as though he's always lived here.

Within a minute Margaret and I are looking out over a field of grazing horses again, with only the occasional wisp of steam rising in the cold morning to give away the fact that they've done anything to raise their body temperature.

"Still worried he'll be cold?" she asks.

I clear my throat. "I think he'll be OK."

***

Back at the house Justin and Lief are raking. Sort of.

Justin makes a pile, Lief leaps into it half-a-dozen times, then Justin re-rakes the scattered leaves.

"The big guy all settled in?" Justin asks.

"Yup."

He gives me a funny sideways look. I realize I should sound happier. It was just a little bruising to my ego when I called out to North before I left and was completely ignored.

Well, not completely. The friendly little horse from my last visit walked over for a head scratch.

I force a smile. "He's all good. Happy as can be. What are you guys up to?"

Lief tackles my leg. "Gil's gonna build me a new seat in my room. One in the window so I can sit on it and it'll have drawers underneath for my toys. I'm gonna help him."

"Oh, really?" I ask.

Justin answers. "Gil's doing a woodworking co-op at the high school—he wants to take the heritage carpentry program at the college. I thought window seats would work well in your bedrooms here. If you want one, that is. He's going to start with Lief's room."

The snarky part of me that was just rejected by my horse makes me want to reject somebody, too. I open my mouth to say, *"No, I'm fine ..."* then I look at Justin's smile, and I picture the comforting view out the tiny window in my room, and imagine sitting there, reading a book. "Sure. That would be nice. Thanks."

"Whoo-hoo!" Lief yells. "I'll help build yours too!"

Please no, I mouth to Justin, and he laughs. "Nobody's going to be helping build anything if we don't get the horse trailer back with our toolbox in it."

"Oh. I can come back with you to get it," I say.

"Have you emptied North's things out of it?" Justin asks.

"Yes. Margaret gave me some space in the barn."

He waves his hand. "Then don't worry about it. Lief and I will drive the SUV over there and hitch it up. You don't need to come along." He gives me a full-on grin. "This is one of the main reasons for living here, Perry. To simplify all our lives. To give you more free time." He punches my arm. "Have some fun, kid!"

Great. Fun. Sure.

He's waiting for me to answer. I shove my thumb up in the air. "Will do!"

Then I go inside and climb up to my room and stare out the wavy-glassed window until I can't tell if it's the glass or the tears blurring my vision.

Chapter Fifteen

I'm used to Sundays being frantic. Used to getting to the barn, still-yawning, asking Karen, "I wonder what it's like to sleep in on the weekend?" before getting totally immersed in either show preparation: re-doing rubbed-out braids, scrubbing at rubbed-in manure, or persuading reluctant loaders onto the trailer, or everything else a busy barn Sunday brings with it: showing horses to potential buyers, helping students get ready for lessons, and schooling naughty horses.

Today I could sleep in, but I don't. I'm up, and wide-awake, and I try to push away my empty feeling by running, hard and fast, through the crisp country morning.

When I get back Justin's created the almighty mess he always generates when he's making pancakes. The flour's out—not just out of the cupboard but out of the bag and liberally dusted everywhere. Along with many other baking products I happen to know don't go in pancakes. There's a near-empty bottle of maple syrup in front of my brother, and he's trying to twist the top off a second one. "No, Liefy, don't open that one until we finish the first one!" Justin dives for him, and I slide into Justin's abandoned spot by the griddle and flip the pancakes.

I try not to count how many egg shells are scattered on the counter.

Justin turns back to me. "Shoo! I'm cooking breakfast. You have a shower, then come eat."

"Do I have to?"

He claps a hand over his heart, leaving a floury outline on his dark shirt. "Perry, you wound me."

"I guess I'm just hoping you'll actually flip my pancakes at least once while I'm in the shower."

"I know what I'm doing."

"The number of egg shells would suggest otherwise. You do know the recipe only calls for one egg, right?"

"My pancakes are delicious. Aren't my pancakes delicious, Lief?"

Lief wipes his finger around his plate and licks it off. "The syrup is delicious."

"Ha! I rest my case!"

Justin snaps a tea towel in my direction, and I scoot toward the shower. "I'll be back!" I call over my shoulder. "Save some syrup for me, Lief ... I'll need it!"

I close the door, push my back up against it, throw my head back and stare at the ceiling.

I'm pretty sure Justin thinks I'm OK. I feel like I pulled it off.

I wonder how much longer I'll have to fake it.

'Til you make it.

It's what my mom said the first time she put on a wig so she could go out for dinner with Justin. The bottom drops out of my stomach as I picture her in their bedroom in our old house, with the big spruce tree rubbing its boughs against the window, and the cracks in the old plaster of the ceiling which looked like the outline of a unicorn. She looked into the mirror above the dresser and smoothed the hair into place, saying, "Sometimes you just have to fake it til you can make it."

The wig was everything her normal hair wasn't. Dark, pin-straight, and so shiny I both wanted and didn't ever want, to touch it. "You're super-glam," I'd said.

"I'm a bald-headed woman who's had to draw her eyebrows on to go out for dinner."

I shook my head, opened my mouth to protest, then stopped. Nodded. "I get it. Faking it."

"Like a pro."

Now it's my turn.

* * *

With my stomach full of rather dense pancakes, I wave good-bye to Justin and Lief at the end of our driveway.

They have some plan or other that involves Gil again.

Poor Gil. I wonder how hard he has to fake wanting to spend time with my little brother.

There's a lingering taste of maple syrup on my tongue, which is actually quite delicious. Overhead a very late vee of Canada geese flies south. Silhouetted against the searing blue of the autumn sky they're as iconic as it gets. And I'm going to see North in a few minutes—no Sunday morning alarm clocks or fear of illogical traffic jams involved.

Maybe the faking is working. Maybe everything will be just fine.

When I get to the gate North is at the back of the herd.

It's fine. I try to pretend it's fine. I fake it.

But he knows I'm here. I know he knows I'm here by the ear cocked in my direction and his careful refusal to look in my direction. He gets like this every now and then, and normally I laugh it off.

I'll come back from the paddock without my horse and Karen will say, "That independence streak surfacing again?" and I'll nod and say, "Apparently the grass is extra-lush today," and Clara will say, "All the more of your time for me—I've got at least three horses you can ride this morning."

This morning no Karen, and no Clara to make me feel better about no North.

Just in case I'm wrong—in case I'm letting negativity get the better of me—I step through the gate. When I look out at my horse, he's doing his quiet-but-definite get-lost manoeuvre. It involves lining his backside up squarely with my line of vision.

I already know if I move to one side, or the other, he'll shift, too.

Normally it's funny. Today it cuts me to the quick. Everything is not fine after all.

While I'm standing, letting pity swamp me, thinking how I left the best barn I've ever ridden at so North could live here and be happy and now he doesn't want to know me, there's a nudge in my back.

I turn around—not quickly; never quickly around horses—and find the front end of three horses facing me. Three very small horses. Foals about seven or eight months old I'd guess.

Wow. Canadians make cute foals.

"Hey guys ..." I hold out my palms and the medium-sized one—the nudger, I'm pretty sure—pushes his nose into my hand. No hesitation. No fear.

The smallest takes one step forward, then stops. The biggest steps back and adds in a snort for good measure.

Well, OK. Now I'm clear on everybody's personality.

I reach into my pocket and pull out the jelly scrubber I found in the back seat of the car. I hadn't been able to locate it when I unpacked the trailer and I was so happy when it showed up. There's nothing North likes more than having his itchy spots scratched. When he deigns to acknowledge me, that is.

I slip the jelly over my hand and look at the fuzzy black foal. "Maybe you're itchy instead?"

I let him sniff the jelly. He seems to think it's OK, so I hold it against his neck and rub it in the lightest of circles.

He stands still. He's got slightly flared nostrils, faintly splayed forelegs, and alert ears.

The other two watch—one leaning forward with interest, the other leaning back in apprehension.

My bold foal decides he likes having his itches scratched and leans in.

"Good boy."

I forget about North as I work my way around the foal's sturdy little body. His muscles are strong and close under his skin. I find a couple of unique whorls of hair, and a healed-over nick on his chest. "Already collecting battle scars, my friend?"

I loosen dead hair, and dust, and some caked-on mud.

Whenever I come to a leg, I run my hand down it. His tension the first time I do it tells me this isn't something he's used to, but by the time I start the second round of moving my hand down his leg, and applying just enough pressure for him to notice, he's got the idea. He lifts his hooves and I tell him he's so smart and scratch one of the extra-itchy places I've found.

The second foal has come close enough to bump my hand and I say, "You want a turn?"

"What are you doing?"

The edge in Margaret's voice sends the timid foal whirling off to find his mother, and the interested foal snorting and stepping back.

The foal I've been handling takes a step closer to me to fit snugly against my side.

Her tone tells me she's already decided what I'm doing, and she doesn't like it. Given that, I'm not sure what to say.

I settle on, "What, exactly, are you asking about?"

"Don't touch my foals."

"Excuse me?"

"This is my farm. Those are my horses. I breed them my way. I don't need a city girl coming in with big horse-training ideas breaking my foals before they're ready."

I'm back to not knowing what to say. Back to feeling miserable and very alone.

I wish Karen was here. She'd tell Margaret I would never, ever, hurt any horse let alone her precious foals.

I wish Justin was here. He'd say, "I'm sure there's been a misunderstanding. I don't think there's any need to get upset."

I wish my mom was here.

Then again, if my mom was here this would never be happening.

Interestingly, North *is* here. He walks up, nudges me, and snorts at the foal tucked under my arm. Now that another horse has noticed me, I'm no longer chopped liver.

I don't need this.

I don't need Margaret telling me off. I don't need North being first sulky, then jealous.

I give the foal a little squeeze and a pat. "You're a good boy."

I turn to Margaret. I don't entirely succeed in keeping the shake out of my voice. "I actually don't believe in *breaking* horses. Just *teaching* them. I'll make sure I only teach my own horse from now on."

Then I turn to North and snap my fingers. "You! Enough of your silliness. You come with me!" I walk toward the gate and North gives a rattling exhale and follows me, and I open the gate, and let my horse through without snapping a lead rope on him, or acknowledging Margaret.

***

I take him into the round pen.

I don't ask for permission.

He's my horse, and I'll use my big horse-training ideas on him if I want.

So there.

"Walk on," I tell him. He doesn't just walk—he strides out, tracks up, arches his neck. He's decided to please me.

I take a tiny step forward and say "switch" and he does that easily and smoothly, looping out in a tidy reverse and heading right back to the outer track, still in his nice lively walk.

The anger is still boiling inside me. *How dare she? She doesn't know a thing about me. I wasn't hurting those foals. I would never. I ... I* realize my fists are clenched and so is my jaw.

"Trot."

North does it, bless him. He can be moody, but he's never a slacker. He deepens the arch in his neck as though to offset the chop of his stride. Remorse pangs in me. "Canter."

He's happy to do that. It's the pace he's most comfortable in. He looks light, and swingy, and easy. He floats.

I watch him go and count along with his one-two-three rhythm, and the anger ebbs out of me.

North is what he is. I've always loved him for that. It's petty of me to be intolerant just because I'm having an off day.

"Walk."

He's voice-trained to perfection. In two strides he's walking.

"Here." I hold my arms wide and he turns and walks in. He presses his face against me, and I wrap my arms around his big head and whisper in his ear. "I'm sorry. I love you just the way you are."

* * *

I walk into a house full of men's voices, and laughter ... and also men's boots. Taking up all the space on the miniscule boot mat in the narrow front hall.

The huge steel-toed boots I noticed on Gil's feet the last time we were here are next to Justin's. Justin's boots—although technically classed as "work and safety" boots at the expensive store he bought them from in the city—look very much like they were bought from an expensive store in the city. I wonder how long it'll be before he replaces them with a pair of practicality-trumps-style ones just like Gil's. Wedged onto the tiny bits of remaining real estate around the bigger boots are Lief's new rubber boots which, even better than unicorns, sport a pattern called "winter birds," featuring chickadees, cardinals, nuthatches, and more.

I can only imagine how proud Lief felt to put his favourite boots next to Gil and Justin's big boots. I'm sure he's having the time of his life upstairs with them, measuring and planning his new window seat.

And I can't find any happiness in my heart for him. All I can think is how terrible the entrance to this house is.

How much I miss the big, custom-designed cubbies and lockers my mom had installed at the side entrance of our old house. How ridiculous it is that anyone would manufacture a boot mat this small. And how mean it is of Gil, and Justin, and Lief to take up all the space on it.

My paddock boots, as always, are liberally adorned with many substances that shouldn't be inside the house. I'm holding a bag in my hand, which I used to carry carrots over to Margaret's. I don't want to put the bag down, and I don't want to touch the boots, and normally they just slide off my feet, but today they won't, and there's nowhere to put them anyway, and I'm muttering, "That's just fine. Take up all the space. My boots don't need to go anywhere ..."

I hear a creak and look up to find Gil, standing on the bottom stair, looking at me. "You OK?"

I freeze, standing on one foot. "Fine. Why wouldn't I be?"

He shrugs. "It looks like you're having trouble getting your boots off."

Mostly because your big boots are taking up all the space in this tiny hallway. "I'm fine."

"Oh, wow. My boots are taking up way too much space there. Here—" He leans forward and lifts them out of the way. "I'll put them on the front doorstep once you have yours off."

A bit late for that. "I said, I'm fine." I bite my teeth tight together and speak through them. "Really."

He bends down and grabs the heel of my boot. "Here. Lift."

"I ..." *I don't want to. I want to do it myself. I want to be left alone.* The deeper truth is, I'm afraid I might cry.

My foot slides out of the boot. *Thank you, Perry. That's what you should say now.* "I would have been able to do it by myself."

He shrugs. "Of course. This way it was just a little faster. And now I can get past you and put these outside where I should have left them in the first place."

While he's bending over to set his boots down outside, I bolt. My sock feet don't make any sound on the wooden stairs. I dash into my bedroom, and press my head against the window, and think of working with North earlier—of me realizing it was petty of me to be intolerant just because I was having an off day.

I got past that with my horse. I admitted my mistake. I acted like a grown-up.

Too bad I can't do the same thing with an actual human being.

I was already finding today difficult, and now it's worse, and the only person I have to blame for that is me.

Chapter Sixteen

Every morning I wake up and run through some of the most beautiful landscape this beautiful province has to offer.

At the end of my run I drop in to see North—no driving required, or traffic jams to battle. When I go to the gate, the rest of the horses step aside to give North an unimpeded path to the fence—and the carrot I bring—and it's clear he's settled. Unlike Margaret and me, who have power issues to sort out, the rest of the horses have ceded their power to North.

It's because of those power issues that I only come in the morning. I'm dodging Margaret. The memory of her words still stings. I don't want to face her.

North's coat is already thicker than it was at any point last winter—when I press my hand into it, the outline stays for a second before disappearing—and the way he's eating it's not going to be just winter hair covering his ribs.

The entire back of Margaret's barn is an open run-in providing good shelter from the prevailing winds, well-drained sand underfoot, and strategically placed salt licks.

I was reluctant at first to allow North to live out, but Margaret showed me the run-in and said, "He's not going to get cast in there."

So my horse is eating, self-exercising, has shelter when he needs it, and doesn't have walls around him to kick or get cast against.

All good. All completely low-maintenance.

Unlike at Clara's, there's no barn full of other horses who need vices worked out of them, and lessons taught to them, and I'm definitely not supposed to touch Margaret's horses ... so, after North gives me an affectionate bump with his nose, accepts a carrot, and wanders back to the edge of the grazing herd, there's nothing else to do except run home.

At the breakfast table I listen to Justin and Lief chatter about their excitement for the day ahead. "I'll walk you to school," Justin tells Lief. "Then, after school I can come see your new office, right?" Lief asks Justin. Or the library. Or the community centre where Lief's already signed up for Beavers. The two of them are definitely happy.

Each morning I eat the perfectly fried egg Justin sets in front of me—another gift from Gil's chickens. It has a yolk the colour you never see from supermarket eggs, and is placed on grain-filled bread from the Water Street Bakery, and I always find it hard to swallow so, when Justin goes into the bathroom to help Lief brush his teeth, I scrape my breakfast into the compost and stir it up so Justin won't see the egg sitting on the top.

I ride my bike to school and I know I'm lucky to be able to do that. The girl who has the locker next to me is nicer than she needs to be. When my English novel hits the floor, she bends over to pick it up and hands it to me. "Hi! My name's Cass. Do you have English now? I do too. I'll show you the quickest way to the classroom and there's an empty seat next to me."

I smile, because I know it's the right thing to do. Really, though, her picking up my book is just reminding me how nice Gil was to me, and how shitty I was to him. Her being nice to me is reminding me how Sata used to be nice to me, and how I succeeded in pushing her away. I follow Cass to class, and sit next to her, but when the bell rings, and she drops her own book on the floor, I don't wait for her to pick it up. I just head out.

Which seems silly when I get home to our empty house.

With Justin using his new flexible work hours to walk Lief to school and make us dinner after work, my evenings stretch very long, and empty, and chore-free.

One evening, as I'm wiping down the not-very-dirty countertop, Justin says, "I told one of my older patients I'd stop by and make sure she understands when to take all her medications. Could you …"

I've interrupted before he can finish. "Of course. Go. I'll give Lief his bath."

I sit on the floor in the bathroom doorway and remember the last time I did this. In our old house. Surrounded by memories of my mom—the beadboard she meticulously sanded and re-painted, her brand of body lotion still on the vanity, the empty spot where her bath towel used to hang that none of us had taken over.

"Perry?"

I turn to Lief, sitting in the bath, pouring water back and forth between one cup and another. "What is it, Liefy?"

"Did you see her?"

My heart stops beating, then restarts in double-thump time. Maybe everything's not lost. Maybe my little brother can help me reconnect with my mother, even all these kilometres away. My voice is breathless. "See who, Liefster?"

"The little bunny who lives under our front porch. She hip-hopped under there when Daddy brought me home from school."

I swallow hard. "Oh, um, yeah. I think I did see her. Long ears and a puffy bunny tail?"

Lief laughs, "Silly Perry, that's what *all* bunnies look like!"

"Hmm ... yes, you're right. But this one was carrying a little basket full of carrots across our lawn, so I'm pretty sure she lives under our porch."

"She was *not* Perry!"

"Well, can you imagine she was?"

Lief scrunches his eyes shut, tilts his head back and twitches his nose. "I can imagine that!"

"Good for you, Lief. You have a most excellent imagination." I'm glad he does, but I'm also sad his imagination doesn't seem to be straying to our mom these days.

I'm sad for both of us.

The front door opens and a swirl of cool air reaches me. Justin calls out, "Thanks Perry! I can take over in a minute so you can do your homework!"

Later, he knocks on my bedroom door. I look up from the book I'm trying to get lost in. "Yes?"

"So, how's school been going?"

Smile. Make eye contact. "Good. They fit me into all the classes I need. I'm ahead in Chemistry, and it's easy to pick up English. The girl who has the locker next to me is really nice."

He smiles back, but it doesn't look natural and, for the first time it occurs to me maybe he's forcing his smile, too. "Everything else OK?" he asks.

"Of course. Yes. Great." *Talk to him.* I know I should. I know I could. Justin listens. He's great. This, though …

I wanted him to be happy, and he is. I wanted everybody else to be happy. I'm glad they are.

I was afraid I wouldn't be, and so far I'm not, and I can't think of any way to tell Justin that without some implication of guilt. Of his happiness coming at my expense. And he definitely doesn't deserve to feel guilty.

He's turning away, and if I was home, I'd get up and follow him. I'd go downstairs and pull out my mom's battered old cookie sheet, and get all the ingredients from their spots so familiar I don't really need to look as I reach for them, and I'd mix my mom's famous chocolate-chip cookie recipe together from memory, and bake it in the oven for ten-and-a-half minutes *exactly* so the cookies are crispy on the edges and gooey inside—but the cookie sheet isn't unpacked yet, and the baking ingredients are just shoved in the cupboard in a jumbled mess, and Justin had to put our dinner back in the oven for an extra ten minutes tonight because it wasn't quite hot enough, so goodness knows what the temperature situation is with Aunt Isabelle's ancient oven.

Bottom line, now not only is my mom gone, but the last remaining comforts I used to be able to cling to are gone, too.

Justin's nearly closed my bedroom door, when he pushes it back open. He clears his throat. "I thought you'd be spending more time with North."

I meet his eyes. "I see him every day."

He clears his throat. "You can talk to me, you know."

I come so close.

There's a sting in my throat and a tingle in my eyes and it takes all my internal fortitude not to cry.

There's a balloon of pressure under my breastbone, and the word, "*Actually ...*" on my tongue, and if he asked again, I'd tell him. All of it. Everything. And there would be crying.

"Just remember that, OK?" This time he pulls my door all the way shut.

I know I could still go after him. I know he'd listen.

But maybe it will get better. Maybe I just need to be patient.

Maybe I can wait it out, and it will all go away, and I won't have to make Justin feel terrible.

I take a deep, shaky breath.

I'll wait a while.

Chapter Seventeen

How long? I'm wondering.

How long should I wait until I feel better?

And what else can I do?

I pull a turquoise-painted wooden chair away from the kitchen table and use it to reach the baking cupboard. I arrange all the supplies as well as I can.

I can't get them the way my mom had them at home, because the cupboard is a different shape, but surely it's good enough to try? To organize them as best I can? To imagine how she'd line them up if she was here?

I wash the battered cookie sheet and line it with parchment paper.

When I bake the cookies I turn the oven light on and watch like a hawk, trying to tell by sight when they're perfectly done.

When we eat them after dinner Justin and Lief make appreciative noises and Justin says, "Perfect. You always make these exactly the way your mom did."

I smile. It's kind of him. The cookies are good, but anyone can taste they're not the same.

Still, Justin seems relieved. He lays his hand on my shoulder. "Good to see you baking again."

At least the passing time seems to be working for him.

***

You'd think my breaking point might come when I'm in the office waiting while the secretary photocopies my little yellow vaccination card to prove I'm safe to have in the school and a woman standing next to me, who actually looks quite a lot like my mom, smiles at me, holds up an insulated bag, and says, "Your mother's lucky to have such a responsible daughter; mine can't even remember her lunch."

The secretary makes a choking noise and shakes her head at the woman, who looks confused and worried. I stay much calmer than the secretary. I just smile back. "I hope your daughter appreciates her lunch," and I don't break down.

You might think it would come when I'm in class listening to two girls behind me. "So, you're going to come over tonight for birthday cake?" "If your mom's making her famous chocolate money cake, you know it."

I'm fine, though. I'm happy for the girl sitting behind me. At the end of class, when she jostles me on her way out, I say, "Happy birthday," and she smiles and says, "Thanks!"

It actually starts Friday morning when I'm locking my bike up. The lock is sticking—slowing me down—and there aren't that many students left outside. A car pulls up and before it's even fully stopped, the passenger door flies open and a tall girl flings herself out of the still-rolling car.

"Jessie!" The voice comes from inside the car.

The girl whirls around. "What is it now?!?"

"Don't you leave the car like that. That is so rude."

"Yeah? Well it's also rude to take my favourite jeans, that I was about to wear to school, and put them in the wash ten minutes before I have to leave."

"I told you anything on your floor was going in the wash. This would never have happened if you'd just clean up your room."

"Aarrgghh!" The girl yells. "I'm so sick of you always being right and me always being wrong. I hate you!" She starts to stride toward the school.

"Jessie!"

Jessie pauses just long enough to call over her shoulder. "I do! Just leave me alone!"

The woman calls through the car window. "Well, I love you! Have a good day!"

And that's it. That stupid exchange freezes me to the spot. Not because my mom and I had fights like that. More because we never did.

To be able to yell at your mother that you hate her, you have to be pretty confident she's not going anywhere.

My mom got her diagnosis just as I was getting to the age where I might, conceivably, have occasions where I'd want to yell, "I hate you!" at her.

But I never would have. Never did. Because I was always aware I might lose her. Which I did.

I'm fully aware of how weird it is to be out here wishing I could yell *I hate you*, at my mother, but there it is. I'll never be able to do it and it cuts me to the quick.

I should realize I'm in no shape to go into the building, but all of a sudden the lock gives up and clicks into place, and the warning chimes go, so on autopilot more than anything I push through the door Jessie disappeared into and head to my locker.

Cass is there.

Perfectly nice Cass, who's been nothing but kind to me all week.

Her forehead creases and she says, "Are you OK? What class do you have first? If it's Bio, no worries, Mr. Zito's usually late anyway and you can sneak in the back door of the lab. He'll never know ..."

"Back off," I say.

It's a terribly mean thing to say.

The only tiny defense I can offer myself is what I actually want to say is, "I hate you." Not even to Cass, but those words; they're in my head, and in my chest—they're everywhere in my body, and they want to come out, but I know they're unforgivable, so I settle on the harsh-but-not-hateful alternative of *back off*.

Which, judging from the look on Cass's face, is plenty nasty.

She opens her mouth and, for just a second I think she's going to give me back as good as I gave her. *Bring it on*, I think, because the pain would feel good, and it would make my words somewhat less egregious, but her eyes settle somewhere behind me, and she throws up her hands. "She's all yours."

I turn to face Gil. "Hey," he says. It's not like I know him that well. Still, he's the most familiar face I have in this school. Plus, in my head, he's firmly connected to my family. My uprush of anger is washed away by a tide of sadness. A tear spills down my cheek.

I have to go. And not to Bio.

I have to leave.

It's a good thing I never even opened my locker, because it means I can just turn around again and walk straight back out of the school.

I walk as though I know where I'm going. Which I do. As far as the doors. Into the crisp fall air. Away from people.

After that I have no idea, but I don't want anyone to know that, so I keep up my purposeful strides. Breathing deeply. Walking quickly.

I walk past the bike rack and to the edge of the building. I turn the corner and stop. Push my back tight against the wall. The morning sun is weak these days, and the bricks are cold against my body. The air is cold on my skin. I close my eyes and fill my lungs with country air.

All I want is to be able to get in the car and drive to Clara's and have North and Karen waiting for me there, along with an endless supply of horses for me to school.

Then I want to drive home, back to our old brick house, and know the dishwasher's full, and there's a load of laundry for me to fold, and I'm needed.

Although, while I'm at it, since I'm imagining being able to turn back time, I should probably go even further back. To when my mom was still alive, and I used most of my free time to prepare for Model UN conferences with Sata, and spent the rest of it slowly getting to know Adam.

I should have refinished the mantelpiece with my mom. I should have let her come to one of my Model UN conferences like she always wanted to. I should probably have kissed Adam while I had the chance.

"Perry?" My eyes fly open and there's Gil, standing so close to me, with his high cheekbones, and floppy lock of hair that seems to point right to his beautiful dark eyes, when I've just been thinking about kissing a boy.

I look away from him and he says, "Hey, it's OK to be upset," and I have to let him think that's it because I can't tell him, *"Actually I'm fighting an overwhelming desire to kiss you right now."*

Plus, I *am* upset. Or, definitely *was*. Now, to be honest, I'm just feeling confused, uncertain, and at loose ends. *Again*. It's the story of my time in Perryside and I really don't like it.

"Shouldn't you be in class?" I ask.

He raises both eyebrows.

"Yes, yes." I lift my hands. "Of course I should be, but you could actually go without making a fool of yourself. Unlike me."

"Having a hard time when you're dealing with a lot of stuff isn't making a fool of yourself."

I find I'm able to look at him now. I still think he's quite amazingly adorable, but I have the desire to kiss him under control. "Well, you're very understanding and I do appreciate it but, like I say, don't let me keep you from going to class."

"I'd feel better if I knew what you were going to do."

I sigh. "I was just thinking that if I was home, I'd drive out to the barn and see my horse."

Gil furrows his brow. "Well, isn't that even easier here?"

"The thing is ..."

"What's the thing?"

"The thing is I'm kind of scared to go."

"You're scared to see your horse?"

"No, not that. It's ... I had a disagreement with Margaret. I've been avoiding her ever since. I'm afraid if I go now she'll be around, and I'll run into her, and ..." I shrug. "More conflict is the last thing I need."

Which is when I think about the conflict I've already been entangled in this morning and I'm hit with a pang of remorse. "Oof."

"What?"

"I was awful to Cass."

"Cass is great."

I mime thrusting a knife into my heart. "That makes me feel better."

Gil laughs. "I didn't mean that. Just that she's a good person, and she accepts apologies. She won't hold a grudge."

I nod. "Yeah. OK. I see."

"You see what?"

I see that he likes her. I guess it explains why she's been so inexplicably nice to me, and why she told him I'm "all his" when I was so rude. He must have asked her to watch out for me. I shrug. Smile. "I see that, for some reason, I've been lucky to meet a couple of people who are much nicer to me than I deserve."

"Tell you what," he says. "Since I have a nice-guy reputation to uphold, let me drive you to Margaret's to see your horse."

He's been super-nice to me, and I haven't been spending enough time with North. And, at this point, neither of us are going back in for Biology. I tamp my nerves down and hope Margaret's out on a run to the feed store when we get to the farm, and I say, "OK. I'm sure North would love to meet you."

* * *

Margaret walks out to the round pen while I'm showing off North's tricks. I don't make him do the bowing one, because I'm not sure it's great for his arthritis, but I show Gil how the big horse will follow me around like a dog. How, if I stand on the fence, he'll sidestep over to let me throw my leg over his back. How I can turn completely around—front, side, back, side, then front again—while North stays out on the rail walking steadily forward.

"Can you ride him faster than a walk even without a saddle or a bridle?"

I lift my hand to straighten my helmet, prepare my aids, slide my outside leg back, ever-so-slightly, lift my inside hip, and say, "Can-ter!"

Popping straight into the smooth, three-beat gait is better for both of us. It means North doesn't have to produce his choppy trot and I don't have to try to sit it with his prominent withers just inches in front of my pelvis.

It also looks really cool.

We sweep around the pen a few times with him moving easily and fluidly beneath me, then I tighten my core, say "Walk" and pray for a smooth transition with no throwing-forward-onto-withers lurch.

I scratch his neck when he gives it to me, and say, "Good boy," and I wait for Gil to say something, which is when I turn to find he's talking to Margaret.

Shit.

I shudder to think of her opinion of bareback, bridleless riding. I shudder to think she won't hesitate to tell me. I'm running through the possibilities in my head:

- Circus antics. Beneath the dignity of a fine animal.

- Over-submission. North is only willing to do this because I've somehow broken his spirit.

- Recklessness. How dare I pull a stunt like that on her property?

The last one worries me because, seriously, what if she asks me to leave? What if we have to move North, yet again? My stomach churns. I shouldn't have let Gil talk me into coming. Shouldn't have been so eager to show off once we got here.

Damn.

I slide off North's back, run my hand down his neck and chest. Not hot. He hasn't even broken a sweat.

That's fine, then.

I take a deep breath, roll my shoulders back and down, and walk over to face Margaret. At least Gil's here. She can only say so much in front of him—right? And if she does tear a strip off me, at least he'll be able to empathize.

As I head toward the gate, I try to figure out what to say. "Good morning?" I mean, it sounds a little stiff. "Hello" is usually a winner, but I can't, for the life of me, figure out what tone I should use. Maybe, "Nice to see you?" A disarming manoeuvre.

Turns out it doesn't matter. "Gilbert tells me he's doing some work at your house."

Gilbert? I raise my eyebrows at him. He raises his back.

"Um, yes. We're adding some storage."

"When I heard you'd inherited the house from Isabelle, I was afraid you'd sell it."

"Oh. Well, no. We didn't." It's the lamest, most obvious answer I can imagine giving, but Margaret nods.

"Thank god. There's a terrible woman who comes here in the summers. She liked the location of Isabelle's house. Asked me to tell her if I ever heard it was up for sale. Said she'd tear it down and build a 'riverside retreat.'" Margaret puts air quotes around the words. "Stupid woman leased a horse from me one year—had no idea how to care for it. Had to take it back from her. Can't abide people who don't look after horses properly."

I stiffen—readying to be raked over the coals for the way I've just been riding North.

"Speaking of which—" Margaret continues.

Here we go ...

"The black gelding out there—" I look toward the field where she's pointing at the herd consisting almost entirely of black horses, and grazing so far away there's no way I can distinguish mares from geldings. Still, I nod.

"He was sent here by a horse rescue about a month ago. Some family bought him for their daughter to show on the hunter circuit. She left for university, they got offered a posting in Switzerland, and they couldn't be bothered to try to find a buyer. Just surrendered him to the rescue, along with a big donation cheque. They passed him along here thinking I'd have more luck rehoming a Canadian."

"OK …" North bumps me in the back. I put my hands behind me and he pushes his muzzle into them. Although it appears I'm not in trouble for my horse care skills, I'm not entirely sure where this conversation's heading.

"So, you'll ride him?" Margaret asks.

"Excuse me?"

"For the man who's coming tomorrow? He'll want to see him go under saddle—will you ride him?"

"I'm sorry … what man?" I'm wondering if Margaret said it, and I somehow missed it. I'm wondering if she told Gil, and somehow thought I heard, too.

She bursts out in a huge, throaty laugh. "There I go again! I didn't tell you, did I?"

"No … I don't think so …"

Instead of being put off by her laugh, North seems to like it. He steps past me to nose toward Margaret.

"You've got a great old guy here," Margaret says as she straightens his forelock.

"Thank you … about the man?"

"Oh, yes, him. I think I probably told the cat about him. He runs an eventing stable near Ottawa. They're looking for a schooling horse. He knows someone at the rescue who told him this horse they sent me might suit him. He's driving up tomorrow to see him. I figure he's more likely to buy him if he can see him under saddle."

My brain floods with questions. How many years ago did the daughter go to university; when was the last time this horse was ridden? What level did she show him at? Is he quick or slow? Does he have any vices? I settle on what I consider to be the most crucial one: "Should I get on him today so I know what I'm getting into?"

"Goodness, no child. I'm not even sure I have tack that fits him—I'll have to see what I can borrow. Besides, anything he doesn't know, you're not going to teach him today. Also, I'm sure you two need to get back to school shortly." She waggles prominent eyebrows. "Am I right? Just come back in the morning before he arrives. We'll figure it all out then."

I put North back in the field and squint against the bright, near-noon sun, wondering if I can at least get a visual on which of the dark grazing figures I'm supposed to sell to some unknown buyer tomorrow morning.

No hope. I haven't been around Margaret's horses long enough to know them as anything other than dark to North's light. I shrug. *Whatever*, it's Margaret's sale to negotiate. If she thinks tomorrow morning is enough prep time, I guess I need to go with that.

Plus, my rumbling stomach tells me it's coming up to lunchtime.

I swing up into the cab of Gil's pick-up and he says, "So, yeah, I can see she really hates you."

"She did, I swear." It definitely feels odd to be trying to convince someone that somebody else disliked me, but I'm baffled by Margaret's about-face, and I feel a weird lack of closure that the last contact we had was confrontational and now, apparently, we're in some kind of partnership.

"I'm sure she did."

"Don't make fun of me."

He grins at me. "I'm actually not making fun of you. The thing is, Perry, everybody has a run-in with Margaret at some point or another."

"Everybody?"

"Yup. It's a rite of passage. It either gets resolved, or it doesn't. Yours, apparently, is resolved. You're all good." He starts the engine and pulls away. "You've gained Margaret's approval. You're well on your way to becoming an official Perryside resident."

I give him a sideways glance. His hands look strong and capable on the wheel. His mouth naturally rests in a smile.

"I feel better," I say.

"I'm glad."

"Thank you."

"Anytime."

Chapter Eighteen

I f I expected Margaret to be outside waiting for me, groomed and tacked-up horse in hand, I would have been disappointed.

It's a good thing I didn't expect that.

When North comes up to search me for carrots, followed by his band of admirers, there are three or four I think might be the horse I'm supposed to ride today, but an educated guess is as close as I can get.

The good news is there's a saddle and bridle just inside the door of the barn. They look fine, but far from sparkling.

Fortunately, I have rags and saddle soap in my tack trunk, along with a pristinely clean snow-white saddle pad.

Once I've used my fingernails to get the caked-on grass residue off the bit, and I've put just the right amount of saddle soap and elbow grease into my tack-cleaning efforts, the saddle and bridle are better than presentable.

I just hope they fit this mystery horse.

For a big woman, Margaret moves with stealth, so the first I notice is when she's halfway to the barn, leading the tallest of the geldings I scoped out earlier.

Please let his feet be in decent shape, I'm praying. *Please let him have stable manners. Please let him remember how to go under saddle.*

Of course, it was wrong of me to worry about his feet. This is Margaret. She doesn't do fancy, but she does do good basic care. His hooves are well-trimmed and look strong.

I walk out to meet them. "Could I see how he goes in the round pen first?" I ask.

I tense, waiting for a denunciation of my silly city horse-training methods. Margaret just shrugs. "Fill your boots."

Margaret has what I assume is a buggy whip propped beside the barn door, so I pick that up and, once she's let the horse off the lead, and has retreated behind the gate, I set about getting to know him.

"Hey." It's all I say. Just *hey*, then let him decide what to do next. Horses are funny in that it can take a while for them to decide to make the first move, but once they do, they're often quick to make friends.

He takes one step toward me, then another, until he's standing right next to me, then he does another thing horses often do, which is look the other way. As though I'm not here after all.

I crouch, huff air out through my nose and, sure enough, that brings him back around. He reaches his nose out to me and huffs right back. He follows it up with a quick trip around my left ear, hair, right ear, then back to my face again for another reciprocal inhale-exhale sequence.

"Ready to work?" I ask him. I pick up the buggy whip and he heads straight out to the track. This is not his first rodeo.

Thank god for that.

* * *

There's an argument that the half-hour I spend in the round pen could be better spent in the saddle trying to work through the horse's kinks of not particularly liking to pick up the left lead canter, and poking his nose to the outside in the trot.

Maybe someone who made that argument would be right. All I know is by the end of the half-hour the gelding and I have the very beginning of a rapport. That he's not afraid of me. That he's not always sure what I want, but he's willing to try to figure it out.

I can also see how he looks, and what would make him look better.

I know Margaret's not into pulling manes or trimming fetlocks.

Still, a hay wisp goes a long way to whipping a shine into his coat, and his legs look much sleeker with North's boots strapped around them. It only takes me a few minutes to twist his thick mane into a running braid, and a braid also keeps his forelock out of his eyes and shows the broad bone of his forehead.

With the bright white saddle pad and the clean tack, he'll make a good impression when the big-time eventing barn owner shows up.

I recognized his name when Margaret passed it on. Even though my barn never traveled to Ottawa for any horse trials, if we had, it would have been for the ones put on by his stable. He was also the technical delegate for one of the big international events held north of the city.

Eventing people are generally friendly and I hope he's no exception.

He comes in heavy country boots and a thick sweater, with an outstretched hand and a smile. "Neil Marks," he says.

Neil walks around the horse who's just a tiny bit nervous, which is good because it keeps him from cocking a back hoof and letting his lip droop and his ears airplane out to either side.

"Before I see him under saddle, can I see him lunged?"

I nod. "Of course. Absolutely." I lead the gelding back to the round pen, with Margaret and Mr. Marks following, and the horse is relaxed and eager by my side—we've already done this—it's no big deal.

I take him through his paces, up and down through walk, trot, and canter on each rein. He's already quicker to respond to my voice commands this time around, and I'm more tuned in to the body cues I need to give him. A half step toward his head is enough to break him from trot to walk—a full step will make him halt.

All-in-all, for a horse who's been living in a field, and a partnership that started not too much more than an hour ago, it goes well.

"Do you always free lunge him?" Neil asks.

I look at Margaret and she waggles her eyebrows. "Um, yes. Generally."

"He's quite responsive."

"Well, the round pen helps. He knows what's expected of him."

"Great—let's see him under saddle, then."

Knowing what I do about his left canter lead, I'm meticulous with my aids. There's always the temptation to rush—as though getting the canter is a game of musical chairs and the last one who manages it will be out. Even when I'm the only person riding, I have to fight against that instinct to want an insta-transition.

Tell him what you want. Be clear. Make sure he understands. It will take longer—and make you look bush league—if you have to drop back down to trot and ask again.

That last argument is the most convincing. An extra second to get the transition is far preferable to the sewing-machine-trot-of-shame followed by the graceless fumble for the correct lead if I let him pick up the wrong lead when I could have avoided it.

When I've ridden the gelding for about fifteen minutes Neil asks, "What do *you* like about this horse?"

I've ridden horses for buyers before and nobody's ever asked me that. It's a smart move on his part. It makes me like him, which makes me want to tell him the truth.

"Well, to be completely honest, Canadians are pretty new to me." I sweep my arm wide to indicate the field of near lookalikes. "I've already figured out they're easy keepers, have nice temperaments, and learn quickly."

That one's a tiny jab at Margaret because her foals would learn quickly if she'd let me teach them.

I scratch the gelding's withers. "This one's a good size anyway, but he feels even bigger than he is. He has a nice stride and he's strong, without being heavy to ride."

Neil nods. "Alright then. Time for me to feel this big stride for myself."

During my ride I thought I did a half-decent job of putting a soft focus on some of the horse's faults but it's like night-and-day to see Neil Marks ride the gelding.

Somehow, while hardly moving, he persuades the horse to frame up, carry himself with an extra spring to each step, and take the left-lead canter without any time for the lengthy internal monologue I worked through.

Margaret and I lean on the gate and watch him ride. "Nice seat," she says.

"Well, he is a four-star rider."

She lifts, then lowers her eyebrows and it hits me that she was making a joke. Maybe? I'm not sure. I'll take a horse any day over trying to figure this woman out.

The gelding is changing rein through the middle of the round pen as though he's done it his whole life; curving around Neil's leg, bending without over-bending. He looks like a million bucks. Or, at least, several thousand. "How much are you asking for him?"

Margaret looks at me with furrowed brows.

"How much money?" I clarify. "What price do you want?"

"Oh, yeah. I guess he's going to ask that, isn't he? Um ..." She half closes her eyes and moves her finger around in the air, muttering, "hay," and "farrier," then tells me her number.

"Uh, no."

"Excuse me?"

"You can't ask that little."

"He hasn't cost me that much."

"OK, first of all, you can't just figure out how much hay he's eaten and go from there. You took a chance on this horse. You gave him a home and you might have had to keep him for ages. And he's had a good home because of everything you've put into this place over the years. And there are other horses who need to be fed after he's sold—" I take a breath, "—and, most of all, someone like Neil Marks is going to expect to pay way more than that amount for this horse."

"So, he'll think I'm giving him a deal."

I shake my head. "He'll undervalue him. And when he gets this horse home, and sees how well he fits in, he'll bring clients back here to look at other horses, and you need to have the right price point on them or you'll lose money on all those sales."

"All what sales, my dear?"

Don't get into a fight with her. Just state the facts. I shrug. "Well, now, that's up to you, but last night when I was trying to figure out which gelding you wanted to show today, I thought there were about three others who would fit the bill. Obviously it's your decision what you do with them, but I'm just saying selling them as eventers is an option."

Margaret opens her mouth, but before she can say anything, the gelding comes to a smooth, square halt in front of us. "Now," Neil says, "Should we talk money?"

***

We're leaning on the fence, watching the gelding amble back to meld into the herd of carbon-copy Canadians. North lifts his head from the grass, reaches his nose out, and gives him a brief sniff of acknowledgment and acceptance.

"One of these things is not like the other," Neil says.

I smile. "That's my horse."

Neil tilts his head. "There's something familiar about him."

I clear my throat. "He was my mother's. She got him off the track twenty years ago. She evented him for a couple of seasons." Until she had me. And got sick. And everything else.

Neil snaps his fingers. "Something Star."

"Seriously? North Star."

"Wow. He looks great. I can't believe he's still going."

"Well, you don't want to see him trot."

"I really do remember him, though. Lots of horses end up this light, but you don't see many so white when they're young. Your mother had her dressage test right before me at one event. The horse was striking and your mother was a sympathetic rider—she didn't get in his way. Their test wasn't technically perfect, but it flowed." He turns to me. "Honestly, it influenced the way I've tried to ride dressage ever since. Is your mother still riding?"

I'm used to this question. I've learned polite ways of answering that don't make the person who asked feel badly. I'm about to trot out, *"There's no way you could know, but ..."* when Margaret interrupts. "She died."

Neil's mouth drops open and he stutters, "I'm so sorry," at exactly the same time as I say, "Margaret!"

Margaret continues. "She was a lovely woman, and it was a sad thing, and I'm sure the young one here doesn't want to talk about it anymore, so let's just make this deal."

I would, though. I came today to stay busy. To keep my mind occupied. To let working with horses be the healing event it always is. But now, I'm getting a glimpse of more. I'm getting a flash of my mother where I least expected it. I'd like to know more.

It's too late to say it now—Margaret's already talking with her customary bluntness. "Listen, here's what I was going to ask for the horse, but Miss Smarty-Pants thinks-she's-a-horse-dealer here tells me he's worth about double that. I've been thinking about it, and I figure the best thing to do is to just ask you."

Neil arches his eyebrows. I don't blame him. "Unorthodox" is the politest way I can think of to describe

Margaret's negotiation style. He looks at me. "Well, now, I can see the riding style you inherited from your mother isn't the only thing that makes you a good horsewoman. I'd say that price is just about right ..."

"But ...?" I ask.

"But, now I know I could have had him for half as much, so how about I make you an offer right in the middle and anytime you happen to be around our farm you can load that pick-up of yours up with as much of our home-cut hay as you can fit in it? No expiry date on that offer."

Neil's personality mixes just enough quirkiness and bluntness to satisfy Margaret. She nods. "That sounds like a fair deal to me."

"And if you think you might have other eventing prospects, I'd be happy to bring some clients here the next time we do a scouting run."

Margaret's already shaking her head, so I barge in. "I'll give you my email. If you send me a message, I'll let you know if there are any for you to look at."

"Fair enough. Now, any chance I can get a cup of tea while we work out the sale details?"

Margaret grunts. "I'll put the kettle on. But it won't be any weak, watered-down tea. It's going to be properly steeped. And I don't keep sugar in the house."

"You can't make it strong enough for me," Neil says.

"We'll see about that." I can tell Margaret's happy by the tone of her muttering as she turns toward the house.

As Neil takes the first step toward following her, I clear my throat. "Excuse me?"

He gives a slight nod, then waits.

"Do you really think I ride like my mother used to?"

He pauses long enough that I believe he's actually thinking about his answer. "Yes. I do. I think you're a little more forceful though. I could see that horse today wanted to lean on your left leg but you weren't having any of it. You ride with a nice combination of empathy and strength."

Before I can thank him, he continues. "If you like, I can put you in touch with the photographer who shot most of the events at that time. That's just when digital photography was coming in. She might have some archived shots of your mother she could send you."

I feel another flutter of hope. It's a connection that might be nothing—but then again it might be something great. "That would be really nice of you."

He smiles. "My brother died when I was about your age."

"Oh. I'm sorry."

There's so much I could ask him, but in some ways I don't need to ask him anything at all. *I get your loss*, he's saying. Which, actually, says everything.

Chapter Nineteen

After Neil leaves, I just have time to groom North and promise him a hack tomorrow before I have to hurry home.

"Where are you off to in such a rush?" Margaret asks. She says it like I'm shirking on work I owe her—not like I just helped her get several thousand dollars more on the sale of the gelding out of the goodness of my heart ... or at least, because I didn't really have anything else to do. "Hot date?"

"Something like that." It's a casual answer, because I can't be bothered to explain that in Justin's new practice each of the doctors works one Saturday a month so patients who have trouble getting to appointments during the week can come on the weekend, and that today I promised to take Lief to the library for story time while Justin works.

Besides, it does feel a little like a date to have library plans with my little brother again. It's another little snatch of normalcy. A ray of sunshine.

"Mmm ... yes. That Gil's handsome alright." Margaret tilts her head on the side and squints. "Although, you probably clean up OK when you're not covered in horse hair. You'd have to if you have any of your mother's genes in you."

My brain fumbles to decide whether to address her erroneous or offensive remarks first. "Gil—" "My mother—" I shake my head. *Breathe. Start again.* I smile. "Guess I'd better get home and start on the clean-up, then."

A little part of me daydreams about how nice it would be to be getting ready for a date with Gil, but when I step in the door and Lief flings himself at my legs half-yelling, half-singing, "I'm goin' to the library with Perry!" I laugh, and lift him up, and kiss his smooth cheek and sing, "And I'm goin' to the library with Lief!"

***

Gil's at the library.

Not just at the library, but conducting story time which, as it turns out, isn't the kind of story time I'm used to at home, with a kindly older woman holding up big picture books and reading out the words, but rather is Gil telling stories about birds.

Not just any birds, but birds I've seen before.

When we arrive he's holding my old friend the grackle.

There's already a bunch of kids plunked on the carpet in a semi-circle and Lief pulls his hand out of mine, and darts forward then, just in time, remembers *manners*.

I can see the inner tussle he's going through. He wants to be in the front row so badly he's quivering, but Justin, and I, and the librarians, Eleanor and Julia, back at our city branch have drilled it into him so many times—"You can't just push to the front"—that it slows him, even in the face of his overpowering desire to be near Gil, and near Gil's stuffed bird.

I desperately want him to be in front, too. I'm almost positive none of the other kids can possibly care as much about birds—dead or alive—as my little brother. My heart is simultaneously swelling with pride at his selfless-ness, and near-to-breaking that I didn't get him here just a few minutes earlier so he could be front and centre.

A little boy sitting to Gil's right pipes up, "I don't like that bird!" and Gil smiles. "That's OK. I'm sure my friend Lief here would trade places with you."

Lief waits while the boy's mom comes forward and leads him out of the group, then he plunks down in his exact spot.

Phew! I'm pretty sure I haven't said it, but I might have mimed it because Gil's eyes flick to me and he grins.

I settle onto some sort of stuffed cube which makes it clear this part of the library isn't intended for anybody full-grown. My knees are so high I have to wrap my arms around them to keep my balance.

The grackle is in an open-fronted box. Lief watches with fixed eyes and parted lips as Gil reaches in and lifts the bird out. He holds it up and says, "Can anybody tell me what kind of bird this is?"

Lief's hand shoots up. "Oh! Oh! Oh! C'n I say?"

"Yes, Lief, what is it?"

"It's a grackle!"

I laugh and Gil looks at me. *Milkshake*, I mouth.

Gil nods. "It *is* a grackle. Does anybody know anything about grackles?"

Lief shifts from one seatbone to the other.

"Lief?"

"They're a kind of blackbird."

It starts as the Gil-and-Lief show, but the other kids get drawn in when Gil produces grackle colouring sheets. Most of the grackles come out in extremely unnatural— if cheerful—shades of red, and blue, and pink, and purple. Lief doesn't have any competition for the sombre coloured pencils he uses to shade his grackle black, then layer blue and green over top, "Because it's 'ridescent, Perry," he tells me.

At the end of the story time, Gil carefully replaces the grackle in its box, and the box on a stack of other boxes containing birds I've met before—the chickadee, the starling—and some I haven't. Among others, there's a cardinal and a blue jay.

The other kids drift away and Lief plunks himself down in the middle of the carpet, paging through the glossy pictures in a massive book called *The Canadian Bird Encyclopedia*.

"So, how'd the horse-selling go?" Gil asks, at the exact same time as I say, "So, this is where you got all the birds you sent pictures of."

We both laugh, pause, try again—also at the same time. "Thanks for remembering," I say. "I'm glad you recognize them," Gil says.

Now we're both hesitant to say anything. We just look at each other for a long second, until he finally, tentatively, says, "You remembered about the milkshake."

"Milkshakes are good."

"Well, maybe we should get one, then. I mean, the diner's just down the street."

"I, yeah ..." My eyes fall to Lief. Is this a *Let's get milkshakes and your little brother can tag along and have some chicken nuggets*, or is it a *Can someone else look after him so we can gaze into each other's eyes over Chocolate Peanut Butter and Strawberry Banana shakes?*

I'm simultaneously planning how I could make that work—I was supposed to take Lief home but maybe I could drop him off at Justin's office instead—and knowing it's not going to happen because, remember? I figured out that Gil likes Cass, when Gil says, "I don't want Lief to feel left out …"

Which sounds enough like scenario number two for me to interrupt, over my wildly beating heart, with, "I'm pretty sure I can drop him off with Justin."

"Yeah?" He looks hopeful, right? I think he looks hopeful.

"Let me just text Justin."

Gil nods. "OK, and I can help Lief check out his books."

"Great!"

"Great!"

My fingers keep slipping on the screen, which means I'm way too excited for a milkshake in broad daylight with a friend, and also means I've only just managed to send Justin a barely legible message by the time we step out onto the sidewalk.

Lief is between Gil and me—holding my right hand and Gil's left—he's humming, and hopping, and skipping and I look over at Gil and he looks at the same time, and our eyes hit and we smile, and it makes me want to hum too.

We're coming up to the diner so I say, "I haven't heard back from Justin, so maybe we can just walk to doctors' office?" when Lief yells, "Daddy!"

I look ahead. Sure enough, Justin's there. Lief runs to him, and Justin scoops him up and Gil and I stop. "Did you get my text? I hope it's OK. It's just that—"

"I saw Ms. Zito today." Justin's pretty crappy at stern looks, but the look he gives me is as steely as I've ever seen him.

"Oh," I say.

"Yes. *Oh*."

"I can explain."

Justin kisses Lief on the forehead. "I'd appreciate that."

Gil's been looking back and forth between us. "Hey, why don't you two go into the diner and have a milkshake and I can take Lief home?"

No! I don't want to get in trouble, and I really, really don't want to replace sitting in a booth with Gil with sitting in a booth with angry-Justin.

"Yes!" Lief yells. "Yes, yes, yes, yes! You can make me a peanut-butter sandwich, and we can read the Canadian Encyclopedia of Birds!"

Justin raises his eyebrows. "Well, sure. That sounds good, if you don't mind."

"Absolutely not. I love the Canadian Encyclopedia of Birds."

Justin lowers Lief to the ground. "OK then. Perry and I won't be long. I appreciate it." He turns to me. "Shall we?"

"Gil?" We all turn to see Cass. Wow, this just gets better and better. Somebody else I owe an explanation to. "Hey, hi." Her eyes sweep across us, linger on me for a second, switch to Gil.

"Hi," he says. "This is Perry's stepdad, Justin, and—"

"Lief!" Cass says. "I've heard all about you. The best birder in Perryside."

God, why does she have to be so nice?

Lief nods. "Gil's pretty good, too. He's taking me home. You wanna come, too?"

"I could walk partway with you guys."

"OK!" Lief holds a hand out for Cass, and the other for Gil and the three of them walk off in a happy formation, with Cass replacing me, and me standing on the sidewalk waiting to be told off by Justin.

Fantastic.

* * *

The milkshakes are good. I have to admit that.

Although, I'm pretty sure I'd enjoy my Oreo with Brownie Bits more if Gil was sitting across from me.

"So. Yes. I skipped Biology."

Justin sighs. "I'd like to give you points for honesty, but I already knew that, and I didn't find out from you."

I take a long pull on my straw. It's paper. It's only going to last halfway through this milkshake. Note to self: if I'm going to have Perryside Diner milkshakes with any regularity, I should keep a stainless steel straw in my bag. "OK, well, working hard for the honesty points—I also skipped English."

Justin shakes his head. "I feel like any honesty points I'd give you are now wiped out by the 'skipping another class' penalties."

I shrug. "It was worth a try and at least I'm not hiding anything."

He rubs his forehead. "You could earn more honesty points by telling me why you did it."

I look at his hands, my hands, his milkshake, then down into the depths of mine—really anywhere but in his eyes. "I was having a hard morning."

"You don't say."

While I'm still staring at my milkshake, my peripheral vision picks up his hand coming toward mine. He pats my hand, then lays his over it. "Come on, Perry. I know you haven't been yourself. We used to talk enough for me to know when you're not telling me things." There's a long pause, then he says, "I miss you," and the pain in his voice makes me glance up to catch his eyes looking suspiciously red.

I can't believe I moved here to make Justin happy and now I've made him unhappy.

"I miss *her*."

"Well. Now I think we're getting some honesty."

"Not her, exactly. I mean, of course, we all miss her and we always will. It's just a lifelong condition now. But I miss living where she used to live."

"You do live where she used to live."

I knew it. Of course I did. But it still hits me like a lightbulb. Or a slap across the face. This is my mom's first home. If she hadn't lived here, I wouldn't have had the life I've had. If it wasn't for here, my mom wouldn't have known Justin, and what would my life be like without Justin? If it wasn't for this place, my mom wouldn't have met my father and the particular combination of genes and cells that's me wouldn't have existed.

Justin's talking again. "I understand, though. I know what you mean, and you're allowed to miss that house. We were happy there. Lief was born there. It's fair to have trouble leaving it behind. But you haven't left her behind. In fact—"

"In fact?"

Justin takes a long, strawberry-tinted sip. "This is good ... OK, what I was going to say is it's no surprise grieving is hard for you. Of course it's tough for everyone, but your mom, in particular, really struggled with her grief about your father."

"She did?"

"What do you know about him?"

"I ..." I think about it for a few seconds. I know how he died. I know how old he was when he died. I know they met here, in high school. I've seen one or two grainy pictures of him. I look into Justin's grey eyes. "I don't know what colour his eyes were."

"Right," he says. "I'm not surprised. She didn't talk about him. Or, more correctly, I think *couldn't* talk about him. She didn't come back here. She just avoided everything about him—outwardly, at least."

"I never noticed. I didn't miss him. I had you." I'm embarrassed to admit it. It seems so obvious now that Justin's brought it up.

"Don't get me wrong—I've always been glad to be there for you, but ... in fact ... maybe by coming back here, you can not only learn more about other parts of your mom, but you could also learn about your dad."

My dad. Not Justin, but my father. It's a new and interesting thought. "I thought he didn't have any family here?" Because, somewhere along the line I'm pretty sure that was offered out as a reason there was really no need for my mom or myself to visit Perryside.

"You're right. It was quite sad, actually. He was an only child—his parents didn't have children until very late in life—and they both died within a year of each other not that long before he died. But he does have a cousin living in town. In fact, you've probably met him."

I clap my hand over my heart. "Please tell me it's not Gil!"

Justin furrows his brow. "Why would it be Gil—" Both his eyebrows lift. "Oooh ... I see."

I snort. "Well, there's nothing to actually see, given that he likes someone else, but it would still feel icky to think I've had—" I search for a palatable word to use with my stepdad, "—a *hankering* for someone I'm related to."

"Ah, so you *hanker* after Gil?"

"Maybe 'hanker' is a strong word."

Justin winks. "No, I really don't think it is." He abandons his soggy paper straw and plunges his spoon into the bottom of his glass. "All I'll say is, you never know. I liked your mom way back before she even met your dad. I thought I'd completely missed my chance with her ... and we ended up being married, so don't give up on Gil yet."

I look back at him and say. "Hmm ... good story but, to be honest, I'd settle for having a milkshake with him."

Chapter Twenty

As darkness falls a late-autumn storm sweeps in. The house is actually very snug—probably because of the storm windows—but being right on the river, there's no way to ignore the strength of the wind. Especially because all the fallen leaves provide plenty of ammunition for it to lift and whirl through the air, and fling at the windows, along with rattling sheets of rain.

My sleep is fitful. I drift off until the wind builds again and keens at my little window. At one point I get up and stare out and think of the sad story of my father dying out there and my mother being forever damaged by it.

Sometime in the early morning hours the storm moves on, and I fall into my first deep sleep of the night just as the sky greys toward dawn.

I'm woken by a thump to the back of my knees. "Cowabunga!"

"Mmpf! Lief!" I moan.

He scrambles up alongside me and sticks his face close to mine. "Good morning Perry! Can you smell breakfast?"

I sniff. Bacon. And coffee. And I can hear the background murmur of the radio.

"Daddy said I could come wake you up." Lief wiggles around then clomps something onto the quilt covering my back. "I saw a bird outside this morning and I want to show you it in the Canadian Encyclopedia of Birds."

"But, wait. I thought you were waking me up for breakfast."

"Five minutes, Daddy says. So we have time to look at the bird."

"OK." I struggle upright while he flips through the book.

"Here." He points to a page describing the Carolina Wren.

"But Liefy, it says here that this bird doesn't live in our part of the province."

He nods. "I know, but I saw it."

I hesitate. At times like this I don't know the right thing to do. Do I go along with Lief? Encourage his creativity and imagination? Or do I try to help him with reality—like this is really too far north for us to see this bird?

He looks up at me. "I know you think I didn't, Perry, but I really did. I know the difference between seeing real things, and seeing things in my head."

"Oh yeah?"

"Yup. Like I see Mom in my head because I want to."

"Have you seen her here?" I'm afraid to ask him. Afraid of his answer. But I'll never get a better opportunity to find out.

"Perry, Mom's not anywhere anymore. She isn't in a place. She's in me, so I can see her when I want."

"Right." I say it like I believe it. I say it like sometime later on today I'll just decide to see my mom and there she'll be.

Also, as I follow him down the stairs, a little part of me wonders if Lief wanted to see the Carolina Wren, so there it was.

We step into the usual kitchen chaos caused by Justin's weekend breakfast cook-ups and he turns to us, "Morning, Perry. Hey, Lief, on the radio they just said the Wild Bird Centre says birdwatchers should be on the lookout for a Carolina Wren since some were blown in by the storm."

My little brother nods. "Yup." Then he looks at me, and if he wasn't too young and sweet, I swear the look he was giving me would be very much, "See—I told you so."

* * *

As though the world is trying to make up for last night's howling storm, the sky radiates with a blue so sharp it hurts my eyes and sun so bright it brings out the usually hidden variations of colours in the dark coats of the Canadians.

It's a reminder that there are only so many days left before we're buried in snow. In other words, it's a day for a hack. I get North tacked up in all his gear and I can see why Neil recognized him. Saddled and bridled, with boots snugged on him, he looks ready to get to work. To show the world what he can do.

Of course, today what he can do is walk me along the road in the opposite direction from our house. We don't see a single other person, or car. Because I'm on a horse, the other creatures we do see aren't bothered by, or afraid of us.

There's a clearing full of Canada geese. There's a corridor of trees alive with grackles who keep up their chucking and chattering while we ride through.

With the fierce, fiery colours of the maples gone, I drink in the muted landscape of dull orange and brown oak leaves against the silver-grey of sweet, the common reeds swaying along the roadside.

I think back to Claire's. To the busy road I never felt comfortable hacking on, and to the loud construction equipment shattering the peace of the trails. I run my hand down the thick, healthy coat of North's neck.

It's a gift to be here, hacking with my horse like this. "Should we make this a habit, bud?" I ask.

North's ears flick to me, then ahead. He gives a sideways dance. "Yes. Sure. If you want." He goes straight from a walk to a hand gallop and I let him run. Love the wind in my face, and the sound of his hooves echoing into the quiet countryside around us.

He slackens sooner than he used to—I can't deny that—but I also can't deny that he's prancy and his nostrils are flared and he's full of excitement, and life.

So we'll keep doing this until he doesn't want to anymore. And—in the months to come—as long as the plow has been out ahead of us.

As we walk back the sun warms my shoulders and I'm fulfilled.

For the moment.

***

As soon as I turn North out I wonder what to do next. I literally tap my foot on the ground and drum my fingers on the gate.

Working with the gelding—however briefly—trying to show him at his best to Neil; that was a sharp reminder of what my role at the barn used to be. Important. Central. A contributor. Always busy. I didn't know how much I relished it until it was gone.

Now, with the gelding gone and North ridden the only thing left to occupy me is the tack Margaret borrowed for him; I might as well clean it along with my own. I've got the saddles over two sideways-turned bales of hay and a bucket containing water warmed in the rusty kettle in the barn and I'm ready to go.

Margaret comes out of her house, clomps down the stairs, and calls, "Don't bother cleaning that!"

I bite my tongue. I try not to sigh. I don't say, *"Here we go again ..."* But I think it.

When she gets close enough that I can hear the wheeze in her breath from hustling over so quickly, she says, "My friend says we can keep it for a while."

We? "Oh-kay ... but the gelding's gone on trial for at least two weeks."

"Not for him, girl. For that other one."

"Which other one?"

"The other one you thought looked like him. I assume that means he'd be a good eventing prospect, too."

"Um ... well, it's not just what he looks like. It depends what he knows, and what his stride's like, and how will-ing he is ..."

"Mmm—you'd better find out, then."

"Excuse me?"

"What part of me keeping the saddle for you to ride that other gelding did you not understand?"

"I ..." *None of it.* "Like, ride him today?"

"Well I get you might want to do your fancy-ass free-lunging first, but since you have school tomorrow, yes, today does seem like the right time to get some work done."

"Alright. There were a couple horses similar to yesterday's. Did you have one in mind?"

"Pick the one that looks best to you. We're not going to run out of Canadian horses around here."

Right. OK. I put one carrot in my pocket for North and one for … Mystery Horse Number Two. I start walking toward the field.

"And you can groom those foals, too!"

I turn around. "Pardon me?"

"The foals. It looks like they found a burr patch after all—the little troublemakers. Also, if you're looking for something else to do, you can find that burr patch."

I wonder if she has any more jobs for me. Like maybe single-handedly loading a delivery of hay into the loft. Or stripping all the stalls.

I nod. "Yes ma'am."

"Are you making fun of me, girl? Because if you don't want to do it, that's fine with me."

I shift to face her, and a shaft of sunlight falls across my arm, and just like that I remember.

Sun streaming in the kitchen window—a beam lying across my forearm. The kitchen so hot, beads of sweat rolled down the back of my sleep shirt and I couldn't find any appetite for the oatmeal in front of me. Lief in a high chair, red-faced with sweat-dampened hair, screaming and dumping everything he could reach on the floor.

Justin's voice calling out—"The air-conditioning repair guy will be here around noon!"

The doorbell ringing, the dog we used to have barking—everything getting louder and hotter ... and then suddenly a gust of air. Not cold, but soothing. Lifting the hair from the back of my neck. Sending a napkin skittering across the table and making Lief stop, and watch, and laugh.

I turned around to see the oscillating fan from my mom and Justin's bedroom perched on the kitchen counter.

I can't hear my mother's voice saying it, but I remember the words. *"Start with something."*

This morning it was emptiness, boredom, borderline desperation, making me think, *start with something*, just to get going.

Now it's train a new horse, handle the foals, find a burr patch—so much to do, and I just need to choose one of those things and start with it.

I know which feeling I prefer.

"Not at all, Margaret. Just figuring out what to do first."

Chapter Twenty-One

When I come in the front door the first thing I notice is the boot mat.

It's bigger. It's big enough. Justin's new shitkicker boots—the ones he bought from the feed store down at the end of Water Street—sit next to Lief's bird-covered rubber boots, and there's still more than enough room for my paddock boots.

That's a definite improvement.

"Hey! I'm home!" I only realize I said "home" as Lief bounces into the hall.

"Guess what Perry?"

"What Liefy?"

"We have cousins!"

"We do? Tell me about that."

Justin's chopping onions. He lifts his eyebrows at me, because of course he knows that I know that we have cousins. Or, at least, Lief has cousins. Justin's sister lives in Ottawa, about an hour and a half away. Justin's been talking about getting her to bring her two kids out for a visit and I'm assuming that's what's got Lief so excited.

There's a red-winged blackbird colouring sheet on the table, and Lief's climbed back up into his seat and picked up his red crayon. He talks without looking at me. "I didn't know we'd have cousins here, and I really wanted to, because Gil has a cousin, and she's fun, so I wanted fun cousins too."

Justin holds out the pasta box to me and I take it. He's pretty good at making spaghetti sauce, but he can never measure out the right amount of pasta. "When did you meet Gil's cousin?" I ask Lief.

Lief gives one of his dramatic snorts. "Oh, silly Perry. I met Cass yesterday just like you did."

"Cass?" My grip loosens on the pasta box and I have to grab at it to keep it from sliding to the ground. "Cass is Gil's cousin?"

Justin turns around. "Yup. Cass's Mom, Anastasia, is ... oh." His eyes fix on mine. "Yesterday, when you said Gil liked someone else. You thought—"

I swallow. Nod. "I thought—"

He grins. "You thought wrong."

Lief scowls. "I *hate* being wrong!"

I take a deep breath. "I'm so happy to be wrong." I look at the pasta in my hand, then back at Justin. "Do you mind if I only measure out enough for the two of you?"

"If it's for the reason I think it is, I don't mind at all."

I step forward. Kiss him on the cheek. "Thank you! I'll sort out your pasta, then I need to get in the shower!"

***

I pace along the sidewalk outside the diner trying not to look like I'm pacing.

I gaze into the window of the next storefront along until I realize it's a real estate agent and I'm looking at postings of several half-a-million-dollar cottages alongside a commercial warehouse listed at $2.7 million.

I turn away and nearly run into Gil.

"Oh!" we say at the same time.

"I'm glad you came."

"I'm glad you called."

It's all but dark—the remainder of the day's light is concentrated into a pinkish, orangey band between the horizon and the black sky. That fading glow, and the light from the diner, shine in Gil's eyes and all I want to do is stand and gaze into them all evening.

The air's not what you'd call warm—but it's unseasonably mild for this time of year, and I'm dressed for it. Plus the adrenaline coursing through me is doing a good job of keeping any chill at bay. The diner looks so bright, and bustling, and public. I'm not sure I want to go in.

"Should we go in?" Gil asks.

I hesitate. "I know I asked you. And I do want a milkshake ..."

"But it's kind of nice out here?"

"It kind of is."

The light glints off his teeth as he smiles. "I hear you. I know what we can do."

He gets us milkshakes to go, and drives to a spot where we can look into North's field, but Margaret can't see us, then he arranges a blanket in the back of the truck and we sit there, holding our milkshakes, watching the day's final magic light wash over the split rail fence and the field full of horses.

I remember the first time I ran out this way, followed this fence, saw these horses.

Back then I had a Robert Frost poem in my head— "Two roads diverged in a wood and I, I took the one less traveled by, and that has made all the difference."

Tonight makes me think of a different one. "Do you know me in the gloaming, Gaunt and dusty grey with roaming?"

I feel the beauty of this time of day—twilight, dusk, gloaming—whatever you want to call it.

I feel that Gil *does* know me in the gloaming. Or, at least he knew enough to bring me here.

Something swoops above our heads and its silent flight reminds me of how I came to know Gil. "So," I say.

"The birds. I think you were going to tell me about them over a milkshake, which we now have."

"They were my grandmother's."

"Really?"

He nods. "She taught herself taxidermy to preserve them."

"Wow. That's amazing."

"Yeah. She had a little workshop behind the house where she kept them. I used to sit out there while she worked and she'd tell me about the birds. For a long time after she died we just kept the workshop locked with the birds inside, then I started taking carpentry and I got this idea to build those boxes so we could do something with the birds."

I turn and look at him. "You built those boxes?"

"Uh-huh. I started them in woodworking class last year and finished them over the summer."

"If I'd known, I would have paid closer attention, but they looked really professional to me."

He smiles. "I mean, I could probably show them to you again, if you'd like."

"I'd like."

We're quiet for a long minute. Out in the field there's a small disturbance. Somebody offends somebody else and there's a squeal, and a volley of hooves thudding on the hollow ground. When they all settle down again, I'm not surprised to see a tall, light figure right in the centre of where the action was. Good old North.

I shift. Wonder about asking. Figure, why not. "I do have one question," I tell Gil.

"Sure."

"The birds. If they were your grandmother's, did it upset you to give them away?"

"Actually, I felt worse when they were just locked in the shed, doing nothing. By bringing them out I've been able to think about her a lot more and, hopefully, they've made other people happy. Like your brother."

His hand is on his thigh and I suddenly find I really want to hold it. I slide my fingers in under his, and say, "Like me, too."

"Yeah?"

"Yeah. I mean, once I got used to the whole 'preserved for eternity' aspect of them, it was definitely great whenever you sent a photo."

I think of Gil having the faith and the generosity to let go of something important to him—the birds—and how it didn't take anything away from him. I think of how a part of me has resisted being OK here. I sigh. "I'm afraid I've been stubborn and a little dumb."

"In what way?" he asks.

"Even though it was my call to move here—even though there were good reasons to do it—which I acknowledged, I haven't done it wholeheartedly. I haven't let go of our old house, and the memories there. I haven't embraced living here."

"I think you're being hard on yourself," Gil says.

"What do you mean?"

"I think there's only so much a person can deal with at one time. I think you made a big change and you're going through a big adjustment and it might take time for you to be able to be ready to be fully *here.*"

"But Lief—he's doing great."

Gil shrugs. "Maybe because of you?"

"What do you mean?"

"When I was working on your window seat, Justin told me how happy he is to be back here. How it's taken the pressure off him and Lief." There's a snort from the field and another flurry of movement as North moves to a new patch of grass and his pasture mates scurry out of his way. Gil nods toward the horses. "And him, too. I'm no horse expert, but he seems pretty happy for an old horse."

Gil squeezes my fingers. "Justin said none of you would be here if it wasn't for you. So, maybe you did a thing to make everybody else happy and now you need to catch up."

A heaviness in me lightens when he says that. The idea that the best is yet to come. The realization that the people I love the most are OK—which I knew, but somehow seems more poignant when pointed out by an outsider—that my turn might be coming, when I'm ready.

My chin quivers and my chest aches. I think of people being ready, and how Justin said my mom was never ready to come back here. I imagine showing her the impossible light of the sunset. Introducing her to Gil. Standing beside her as she lifted her foot to the split rail fence and looked out across the field full of horses, including her tall, white horse, glowing in the final flare of the sun.

I think she'd be ready now.

I think I'm a little bit more ready.

I turn to Gil. "Would you … I mean … I thought Cass … I thought you and Cass … Lief told me Cass is your cousin …"

I can't blame him for furrowing his brow as he tries to follow my stop-start sentence. As I near the end he says, "Oh … Oh! No. I mean, yes. I mean Cass is my cousin, and you're not …"

I laugh. "I think you're making about as much sense as me. What I was actually trying to say is, I've liked you from the moment I saw you talking about birds with my puking brother."

"I've liked you from the moment I showed you the puke on my shoe and then really wished I hadn't."

"Well, I like the way we met, but if you want, instead of telling people we first met over a puking kindergartener, we can tell them we had our first kiss after drinking milkshakes in the back of a pick-up truck watching the sunset over a field of horses."

"We can?"

I pull my legs in, cross them in front of me, and swivel to face him. "We can if that's OK with you."

He turns and faces me. "It sounds good to me."

We both lean in, and our lips meet, and I giggle. "You taste like chocolate-peanut-butter."

He mumbles. "Sorry."

"Don't be. It's my new favourite."

We brush lips again, and it sends a tingle spreading across my face, and butterflies fluttering in my stomach. From nearby there's a snort, and I think it's North, and I'm about to tell him to leave us alone, when Gil runs his hand along my cheek, then up, spreading his fingers through my hair, and pulls me closer and I'm short of breath, and my head's spinning, and there's no maybe about it—I'm definitely ready to be happy here.

Chapter Twenty-Two

I'm getting used to Margaret. Or, at least, I think I am. Maybe I'm just getting used to not understanding her.

The work with her horses is going well. The foals come to the fence when they see me. The sharpest one has learned to walk beside me. Stop when I stop. Stand still while I walk around him.

The next chosen gelding—Prospect Number Two, as I'm still calling him in the absence of a good name—was clearly never used in the hunter-jumper ring. Or any other ring.

Still, we've progressed. He handles almost as well as the foals now.

I've been here every day after school and spent all yesterday—Saturday—working hard enough to stay warm despite the daytime highs which have stopped rising into double digits. Margaret even brought out two steaming mugs of tea halfway through the afternoon, which we drank as we watched the horses do a lot of grazing and dozing in the late autumn sun while they slowly-but-surely grew their winter coats.

Sunday morning I've just brought North back from our now-weekly hack. I'm turning him out, and scanning the field for my new project gelding, when Margaret bustles out. "That's enough now."

I don't have to look at my phone to know it's nowhere near noon yet. "Pardon me?"

"Goodness, girl. Everyone's entitled to a day of rest. Give that poor stupid gelding twenty-four hours to let his brain catch up with all the things you've taught him this week."

"But ..." This is the same woman who, when I asked if I should start work with the gelding last Sunday, said "Since you have school tomorrow, yes, today does seem like the right time to get some work done."

Margaret has her arms crossed and her jaw set and I guess I know her well enough to know she's not going to back down on this.

That's OK. Before, I would have been lost without the horses to work with. Now I have things to do. Justin brought me a shoe box full of old photos he found on a shelf in the back of the closet in his room. He laid them on top of a stack of high school yearbooks—"We can go through those together if you like." He met me after school one day and introduced me to the guidance coun-sellor, Mr. Menard—"Your dad's cousin," he explained.

Mr. Menard seemed nice. He smiled. "What do you want to know about your father?" he asked. "Probably everything," I said. "Why don't you all come over for Sunday dinner and we can talk?" he suggested.

With these things to look forward to, I clean North's tack, and slip him a final carrot over the gate, and head home.

***

"Justin? Lief?" I don't know why I call their names—I can tell the house is empty as soon as I step in the door. The longer we live here the more it feels like our home, instead of like Aunt Isabelle's house that we just happen to live in.

Of course, it feels more like our home when I can hear Justin somewhere hammering away at a shelf that needs straightening. Or sanding down a door that sticks. Or, in his downtime, strumming away at the guitar he's finally found the time to take up again.

It feels cozy when I have to step over Lief pushing cars along the hall with loud engine noises, or when I have to dodge a full-on charge as he roars through the kitchen as a T-Rex on a hunt.

Empty like this, I see the devil of a dishwasher that I'll never, ever, crack. I notice the thread-worn path right up the middle of the carpet on the stairs. I think how bland the living room is.

I'm much happier about how things are going, with horses to work with, the cutest guy in town to kiss, and a new outlook on my mother's—and my father's—legacy in my life.

Still, I didn't expect to be back here, in an empty house so early.

I sigh. I can handle this. I'll eat lunch. Do some school work. I told Gil I'd be busy all day, and he said he was busy, too, but maybe I'll see him later.

After I eat there are those photos to start looking through.

I'm staring into the cupboard, waiting for lunch inspiration to strike, when my phone buzzes with a text from Justin.

I hate to ask this, Perry, but Lief and I walked up to the school and now he says his legs are too tired to walk home. Could you come pick us up?

Be there ASAP.

I grab the car keys and rush out of the kitchen leaving the cupboard door open behind me.

***

I slow as I approach the elementary school. I expect to see Justin pushing Lief on one of the swings in the playground, or waiting for him at the bottom of the slide.

Nothing. The swings are still—not even swaying from a passing breeze.

Motion attracts my attention to the other side of the road, however. Lief jumping up and down. Justin waving. What are they doing in the high school parking lot?

I slow, turn in, and pull into a parking spot near a truck that looks suspiciously familiar.

I step out of the SUV. "What are you guys doing here?"

Lief runs forward and grabs my hand. "I need to pee!"

"OK. Well we'll get you home quickly."

"No. I need to go now." He tugs at my hand. "You can show me where the bathroom is."

"But, Liefy, the school will be locked." I look at Justin. *Help me out here.*

He shrugs. "Maybe not. Sometimes there are weekend programs."

Lief's putting all his weight into pulling me toward the school. "Fine. We'll try." I start walking. Justin follows us. "Hey," I say as we approach the front doors. "Doesn't that look like Gil's truck?"

"Does it?" Justin asks.

Lief reaches out and hauls on the school door, which cracks open. "See! I toldya!"

I take hold and open it the rest of the way. "You were right, Lief." We step into the main hall. "It's just this way."

"I don't really hafta go."

"Lief!" I turn to Justin with a *Really?* expression on my face, but he just gives me a *whatever* shrug.

"Lief!" The loud whisper comes from an offshoot off the main hall which I've never been down, due to not having any classes there. My brother immediately perks up and starts dragging me in that direction.

"Gil?" I'm sure the voice was Gil's. Which only makes sense in that this is his school, too. But it's the weekend, and he seemed to be expecting my brother, and those things don't make sense at all.

Lief's brought me to a set of double doors that open into a vast, bright space full of large-but-silent machines, with wood stacked along the walls and sawdust floating in the rays of afternoon sun. I look at my three favourite human men, and ask, "What the heck is going on here?"

Lief runs over to a sheet-shrouded item and asks, "Can I do it now, Gil? Can I, Justin? Please, please, please?"

Gil laughs, "Go for it!" and my little brother grabs one side of the fabric and yanks so hard he spins, and the cloth twines around him, and he topples over.

I let Justin go to help him because I'm too busy clapping one hand over my mouth, and the other one over my pounding heart as I stare at the mantelpiece I haven't seen since we moved here.

"What …?" I look at Gil, trying to figure this out, and he says, "I saw it when I helped Justin bring the trailer back. He explained about it being a project you were going to do."

I nod. I blink. My vision's blurry. "With my mom."

He nods back. "Anyway, I got permission from Mr. Kumar to work on a project here this weekend, so if you're up for it—" He points off to the side where I see an assortment of tools, and some tins. "You can tell me what kind of finish you want, and I can point you in the right direction."

I walk over to the mantelpiece and close-up there are so many memories. A split in the wood my mom pointed out back when she was planning the project—"I have no idea what the proper way is to fill that in—maybe I'll just dab on a lot of paint and hope it covers it?" I reach under the shelf and find the hooks she twisted in so we could hang our stockings there. I turn to Justin. "Will it fit in our living room here?"

He smiles. "Sure will. Gil and I measured it."

"Wow …" I turn to Gil. "Super-wow."

"So it's OK?"

I laugh. "It's perfect. I can't wait to get started."

* * *

Justin and I talk it through with Gil. "I wish I'd listened more carefully when she was planning it," I tell Justin.

He smiles. "Your mom was super-organized about everything to do with you and your brother, but when it came to stuff like this, she tended to wing it. I think you don't remember her plan, because she didn't really have one."

"Oh." This further reframes my thoughts about my memories of my mom. Maybe it isn't always my fault I can't remember. Maybe sometimes there isn't a memory there to find. "So, it's up to us to figure it out?"

He nods. "I'd say so. We're the ones who're going to live with it every day, anyway."

"True."

Gil shows us different options—rustic, clean, bright. One of the paints he has is a gorgeous creamy light grey. "I really like that one," I say.

It's not like any of the swatches my mom dabbed on the bottom, but I think if she was here she would have liked the grey one too.

Lief frowns. "It's not very colourful."

"That's because we want to hang your big painting of autumn leaves over the mantelpiece," I say. "It's super-bright and we wouldn't notice it as much if the mantel was bright, too."

Lief squints his eyes as though he's trying to picture it, then copies Justin—"True." A different memory swamps me. A more recent one, from that night when we all stopped in to see North at his old barn.

Now, like then I'm overwhelmed by a sudden wave of peace and happiness, and I think the three of us have got this, and we're going to be just fine ... and then it hits me. This is what Lief meant. My mom's here right now.

"I think that's going to look really good," Gil says. "And I think you have everything you need, so I'll let you get started."

"Wait," I say. "You're not staying?"

"I ..." He hesitates. "I don't want to intrude. This is something for you guys to do together."

I shake my head. "No way. I've learned my lesson. I'm making every memory I can, and I'd really like you to be in this one."

He looks at me, then at Justin, but in the end it doesn't matter what either of us say, because Lief hurls himself at Gil and grabs his leg, and says, "Come on, you have to give me the best paintbrush."

PLEASE LEAVE A REVIEW!

REVIEWS help me sell books. More sales let me write more books. A simple star rating and a few quick words are all that's needed to help other readers decide if they want to read my books.

To review, please follow this link – https://tinyurl.com/ReviewMoNo – and select your preferred retailer. Or, use this QR code:

Chapter One

Appaloosa Summer • Island Series
Book One

I'm staring down a line of jumps that should scare my brand-new show breeches right off me.

But it doesn't. Major and I know our jobs here. His is to read the combination, determine the perfect take-off spot, and adjust his stride accordingly. Mine is to stay out of his way and let him jump.

We hit the first jump just right. He clears it with an effortless arc, and all I have to do is go through my mental checklist. Heels down. Back straight. Follow his mouth.

"Good boy, Major." One ear flicks halfway back to acknowledge my comment, but not enough to make him lose focus. A strong, easy stride to jump two, and he's up, working for both of us, holding me perfectly balanced as we fly through the air.

He lands with extra momentum; normal at the end of a long, straight line. He self-corrects, shifting his weight back over his hocks. Next will come the surge from his muscled hind end; powering us both up, and over, the final tall vertical.

It doesn't come, though. How can it not? "Come on!" I cluck, scuff my heels along his side. No response from my rock-solid jumper.

The rails are right in front of us, but I have no horse-power – nothing – under me. By the time I think of going for my stick, it's too late. We slam into several closely spaced rails topping a solid gate. Oh God. Oh no. Be ready, be ready, be ready. But how? There's no good way. There are poles everywhere, and leather tangling, and dirt. In my eyes, in my nose, in my mouth.

There's no sound from my horse. Is he as winded as me? I can't speak, or yell, or scream. Major? Is that him on my leg? Is that why it's numb? People come, kneel around me. I can't see past them. I can't sit up. My ears rush and my head spins. I'm going to throw up. "I'm going to …"

* * *

I flush the toilet. Swish out my mouth. Avoid looking in the mirror. Light hurts, my reflection hurts, everything hurts at this point in the afternoon, when the headache builds to its peak.

Why me?

I've never lost anybody close to me. My grandpa died before I was born, and my widowed grandma's still going strong at ninety-four. She has an eighty-nine-year-old boyfriend. They go to the racetrack; play the slots.

If I had to predict who would die first in my life, I would never, in a million years, have guessed it would be my fit, young, strong thoroughbred.

Never.

But he did.

Thinking about it just sharpens the headache, so I press a towel against my face, blink into the soft fluffiness.

"Are you OK?" Slate's voice comes through the door. With my mom and dad at work, Slate's been the one to spend the last three days distracting me when I'm awake, and waking me up whenever I get into a sound sleep. Or that's what it feels like.

"Fine." I push the bathroom door open.

"Puke?"

I nod. Stupid move. It hurts. Whisper instead. "Yes."

"Well, that's a big improvement. Just the once today."

She follows me back to my room. She's not a pillow-plumper or quilt-smoother – I have to struggle into my rumpled bed – but it's nice to have her around. "I'm glad you're here, Slatey." I sniffle, and taste salt in the back of my throat.

I'm close to tears all the time these days. "Normal," the doctor said. Apparently, tears aren't unreasonable after suffering a knock to the head hard enough to split my helmet in two, with my horse dropping stone cold dead underneath me in the show ring. I'm still sick of crying, though. And puking, too.

"Don't be stupid, Meg; being here is heaven. My mom and Agate are going completely over the top organizing Aggie's sweet sixteen. There are party planning boards everywhere, and her dance friends are always over giggling about it too."

"Just as long as it's not about me. I don't want to owe you."

"'Course not; you're not that great of a best friend."

***

The way I know I've fallen asleep again, is that Slate is shaking me awake. Again.

"Huh?" I open one eye. Squinting. The sunlight doesn't hurt. In fact, it feels kind of nice. I open both eyes.

"Craig's here."

I struggle to get my elbows under me, and the shot of pain to my head tells me I've moved too fast.

"Craig?"

She's nodding, eyes wide.

"Like our Craig?"

"Uh-huh."

First my mom canceled her business trip scheduled for the day after the accident; now our eighty-dollar-an-hour, Level Three riding coach is at my house. "Are you sure I'm not dying, and you just haven't told me?"

"I was wondering the same thing."

"What am I wearing?" I blink at cropped yoga pants and a t-shirt I got in a 10K race pack. It doesn't really matter – I've never seen Craig when I'm not wearing breeches and boots; never seen, or even imagined him in the city – changing clothes is hardly going to make a difference.

Slate leads the way down the stairs, through the hallway and into the kitchen, where Craig's shifting from foot to foot, reading the calendar on the fridge. He must be bored if he wants the details of my dad's Open Houses, my mom's travel itinerary.

"Smoking," Slate whispers just before Craig turns to me. And, technically, she's right. His eyes are just the right shade of emerald, surrounded by lashes long enough to be appealing, while stopping short of girly. His cheekbones are high and pronounced, just like his jawbone. And his broad, tan shoulders, and the narrow hips holding up his broken-in jeans are the natural trademarks of somebody who works hard – mostly out-side – for a living.

But he's our riding coach. Craig, and our fifty-five-year-old obese vice-principal (with halitosis), are the two men in the world Slate won't flirt with. I don't flirt with him, mostly because I've never met a guy I like more than my horse. Major ...

"Hey Meg." Craig's quiet voice is a first. The gentle hug. He steps back, eyes searching my head. "Do you have a bump?"

I take a deep breath and throw my shoulders back. "Nope." Knock my knuckles on my temple. "All the damage is internal."

Craig's brow furrows. "Meg, you can tell me how you really feel." No I can't. Of course I can't. Even if I could explain the emptiness of losing my three-hour-a-day, seven-day-a-week companion, the guilt at "saving" him from the racetrack only to kill him in the jumper ring, and the take-it-or-leave-it feeling I have about showing again, none of that is conversation for a sunny springtime afternoon.

Still, I can offer a bit of show and tell. "I have tonnes of bruises. And I've puked every day so far. And, this is weird but, look." I use my index finger to push my ear-lobe forward. "My earring caught on something and tore right through."

The colour drains from Craig's face, and now I think he might puke.

"Meg!" Slate pokes me in the back. "Sit down with Craig and I'll make tea."

Craig pulls something out of his pocket, places it on the table. A brass plate reading Major. The one from his stall door. "We have the rest of his things in the tack room. We put them all together for you."

Yeah, because you wanted to rent out the stall. I can't blame him. There's a massive waiting list to train with Craig. And my horse had the consideration to die right at the beginning of the show season. Some new boarder had her summer dream come true.

I reach out; turn the plaque around to face me. Craig's trained me too well – tears in one of his lessons result in a dismissal from the ring – so now, even with a concussion, I can't cry in front of him. Deep breath. I rub my thumb over the engraved letters M-A-J-O-R. "There was nothing that horse couldn't do."

Craig sighs. "You're right. He was one in a million. Have you thought about replacing him?"

If you liked the first chapter of Appaloosa Summer, why not read the rest of the book? You can find it using this QR code

ABOUT THE AUTHOR

TUDOR ROBINS is the author of books that move your heart, mind, and pulse.

A little piece of Tudor's own heart is in many places: the central-Ottawa neighborhood where she lives, the Gatineau hills and Eastern Ontario countryside where she loves to hike, Wolfe Island and the St. Lawrence River where she loves swimming and paddleboarding, and the university towns that are currently home to her children.

When she's not writing, Tudor rides, runs, quilts, and walks with her best friends and her Jack Russell / Potcake mix, Cara.

Please contact Tudor at tudorrobins@gmail.com!

* 9 7 8 1 9 9 9 1 3 3 8 6 3 *